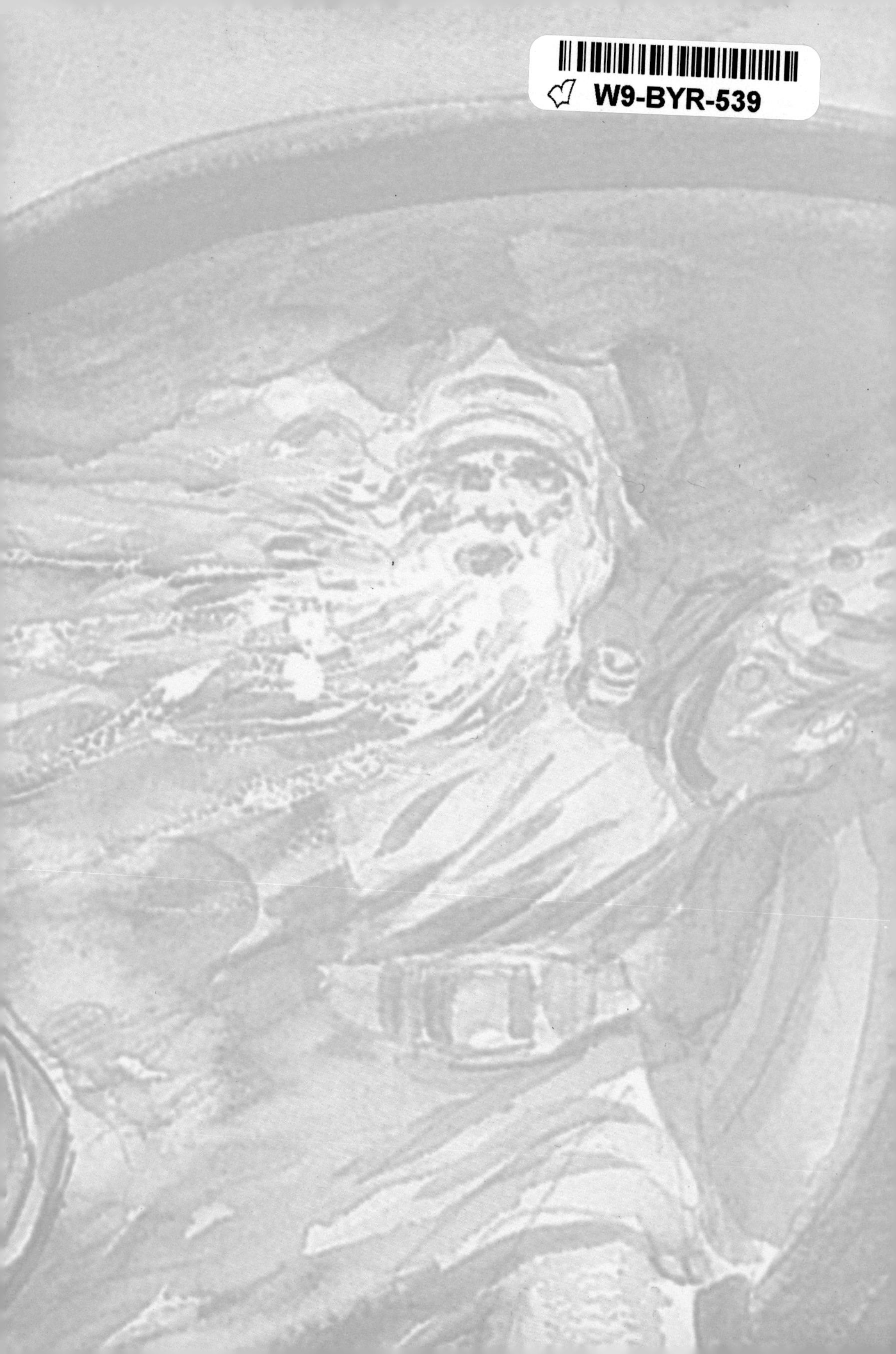

William Shakespeare

HAMLET

adapted by

Steven Grant
writer

Tom Mandrake
artist

Gary Fields
letterer

CLASSICS Illustrated®
Featuring Stories by the
World's Greatest Authors

PAPERCUTZ

CLASSICS ILLUSTRATED GRAPHIC NOVELS AVAILABLE FROM PAPERCUTZ

CLASSICS ILLUSTRATED DELUXE:

FULL-COLOR GRAPHIC NOVEL ADAPTATION
CLASSICS Illustrated Deluxe
THE WIND IN THE WILLOWS
By Kenneth Grahame
Adapted by Michel Plessix
"A VISUAL MASTERPIECE..." -NEWSWEEK
PAPERCUTZ

Graphic Novel #1
"The Wind In
The Willows"

FULL-COLOR GRAPHIC NOVEL ADAPTATION
CLASSICS Illustrated Deluxe
TALES FROM THE BROTHERS GRIMM
Adapted by Mazan, Cecile Chicault, and Philip Petit
PAPERCUTZ

Graphic Novel #2
"Tales From The
Brothers Grimm"

FULL-COLOR GRAPHIC NOVEL ADAPTATION
CLASSICS Illustrated Deluxe
FRANKENSTEIN
By Mary Shelley
Adapted by Marion Mousse
PAPERCUTZ

Graphic Novel #3
"Frankenstein"

CLASSICS ILLUSTRATED:

CLASSICS Illustrated
GREAT EXPECTATIONS
By Charles Dickens
Adapted by Rick Geary

#1 "Great
Expectations"

CLASSICS Illustrated
THE INVISIBLE MAN
By H.G. Wells
Adapted by Rick Geary
PAPERCUTZ

#2 "The
Invisible
Man"

CLASSICS Illustrated
THROUGH THE LOOKING-GLASS
By Lewis Carroll
PAPERCUTZ

#3 "Through
the
Looking-Glass"

CLASSICS Illustrated
The Raven and Other Poems
by Edgar Allan Poe
Illustrated by Gahan Wilson

#4 "The Raven
and
Other Poems"

CLASSICS Illustrated
Hamlet
PAPERCUTZ

#5 "Hamlet"

Classics Illustrated Deluxe are available for $13.95 each in paperback and $17.95 in hardcover.
Classics Illustrated are available only in hardcover for $9.95 each. Please add $4.00 for postage and handling for the first book, add $1.00 for each additional book.
MC, Visa, Amex excepted or make check payable to NBM Publishing.
Send to: **Papercutz, 40 Exchange Place, Suite 1308, New York, NY 10005 • 1-800-866-1223**

WWW.PAPERCUTZ.COM

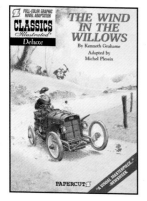

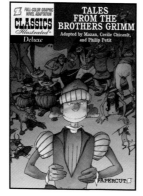

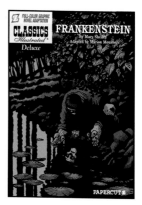

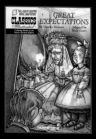

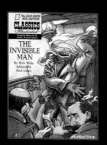

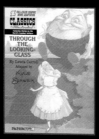

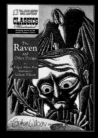

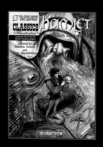

CLASSICS Illustrated ®

Featuring Stories by the World's Greatest Authors

#5

hamlet

By William Shakespeare
Adapted by Steven Grant
and Tom Mandrake

PAPERCUTZ™
New York

The basic story of **Hamlet**, the vengeance-seeking prince of Denmark, pre-dated William Shakespeare's play by at least 400 years. Shakespeare apparently based his romantic tragedy on a version of the Scandinavian legend that appeared in *Histories Tragiques* (1576) by Francois de Belleforest, who in turn seems to have relied on Saxo Grammaticus' *Historia Danica* (1200s). Shakespeare may have also drawn from *Ur-Hamlet* (1580s), a play, possibly by the popular playwright Thomas Kyd, that has not survived. It is impossible to determine exactly when Shakespeare completed **Hamlet** and when it was first performed, but written accounts indicate that the first staging took place before 1602. By the time **Hamlet** was staged by Shakespeare's company, the Lord Chamberlain's Men, he had already written more than 20 highly successful plays. Like his other works ofr the theater, **Hamlet** was written with an eye toward the Globe Theatre's box office; Shakespeare's goal was full houses, not critical success. It is testimony to his genius that Shakespeare achieved both: **Hamlet** was a success from its first opening day, continuing to thrill audiences and readers throughout the years, and is considered by many scholars to be the greatest work of the world's premier playwright. A poetic, compelling tale of revenge, **Hamlet** also is an insightful examination of the complexity of grief, and of the ageless battle between duty and morality. Several versions of **Hamlet** exist; this adaptation is based on what is generally regarded as the definitive version, a combination of texts that were published in 1604 and 1623.

Hamlet
By William Shakespeare
Adapted by Steven Grant and Tom Mandrake
Wade Roberts, Original Editorial Director
Alex Wald, Original Art Director
Production by Ortho
Classics Illustrated Historians — John Haufe and William B. Jones Jr.
Editorial Assistant — Michael Petranek
Jim Salicrup
Editor-in-Chief

ISBN 13: 978-1-59707-149-9
ISBN 10: 1-59707-149-8

Printed in China.
February 2009 Regent Publishing
6/f, Hang Tung Resource Centre,
No.18 A Kung Ngam Village Road,
Shau Kei Wan, Hong Kong
Distributed by Macmillan.

10 9 8 7 6 5 4 3 2 1

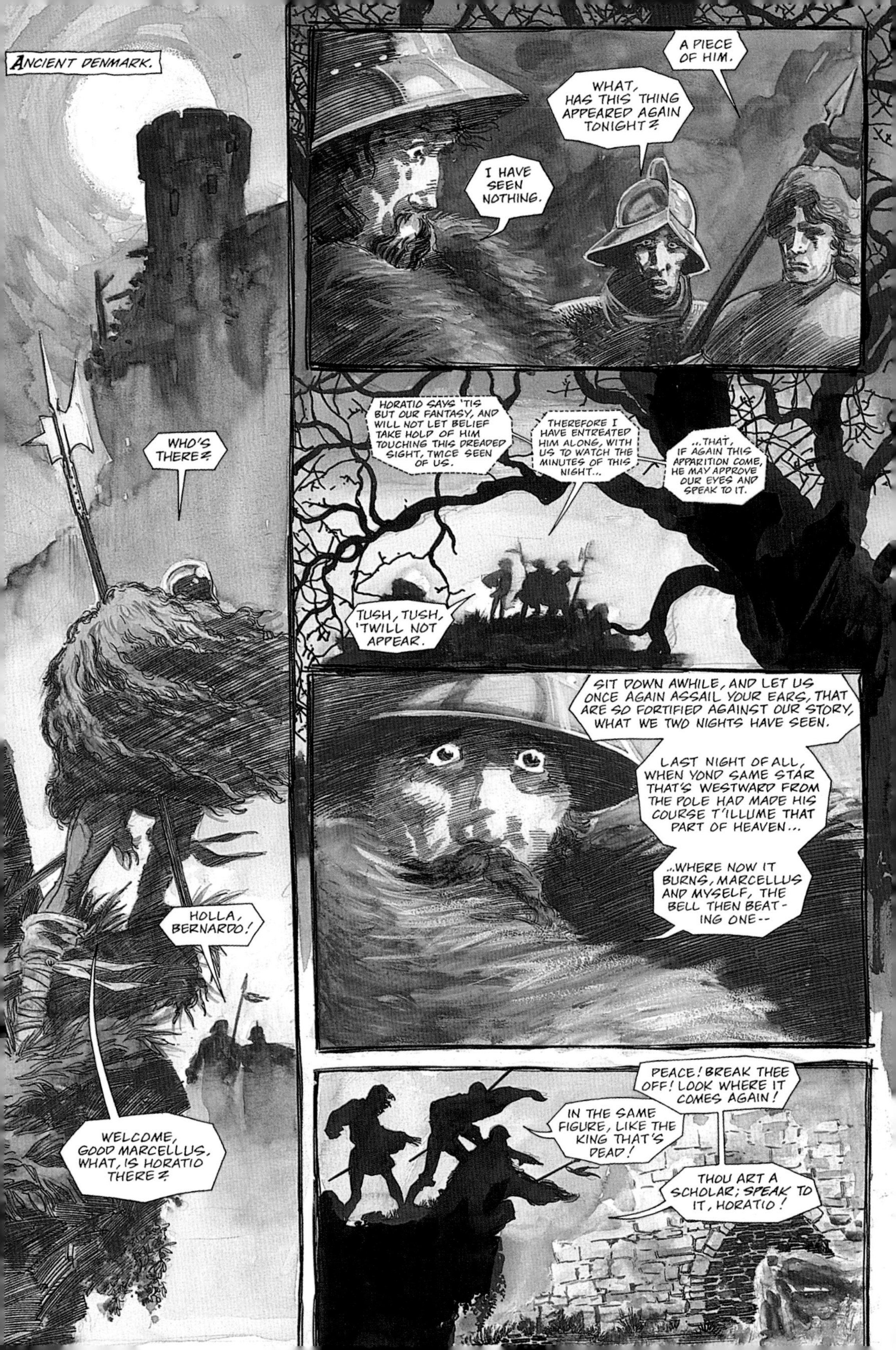
ANCIENT DENMARK.
WHO'S THERE?
HOLLA, BERNARDO!
WELCOME, GOOD MARCELLUS. WHAT, IS HORATIO THERE?
A PIECE OF HIM.
WHAT, HAS THIS THING APPEARED AGAIN TONIGHT?
I HAVE SEEN NOTHING.
HORATIO SAYS 'TIS BUT OUR FANTASY, AND WILL NOT LET BELIEF TAKE HOLD OF HIM TOUCHING THIS DREADED SIGHT, TWICE SEEN OF US.
THEREFORE I HAVE ENTREATED HIM ALONG, WITH US TO WATCH THE MINUTES OF THIS NIGHT...
...THAT, IF AGAIN THIS APPARITION COME, HE MAY APPROVE OUR EYES AND SPEAK TO IT.
TUSH, TUSH, 'TWILL NOT APPEAR.
SIT DOWN AWHILE, AND LET US ONCE AGAIN ASSAIL YOUR EARS, THAT ARE SO FORTIFIED AGAINST OUR STORY, WHAT WE TWO NIGHTS HAVE SEEN.
LAST NIGHT OF ALL, WHEN YOND SAME STAR THAT'S WESTWARD FROM THE POLE HAD MADE HIS COURSE T'ILLUME THAT PART OF HEAVEN...
...WHERE NOW IT BURNS, MARCELLUS AND MYSELF, THE BELL THEN BEAT-ING ONE--
PEACE! BREAK THEE OFF! LOOK WHERE IT COMES AGAIN!
IN THE SAME FIGURE, LIKE THE KING THAT'S DEAD!
THOU ART A SCHOLAR; SPEAK TO IT, HORATIO!

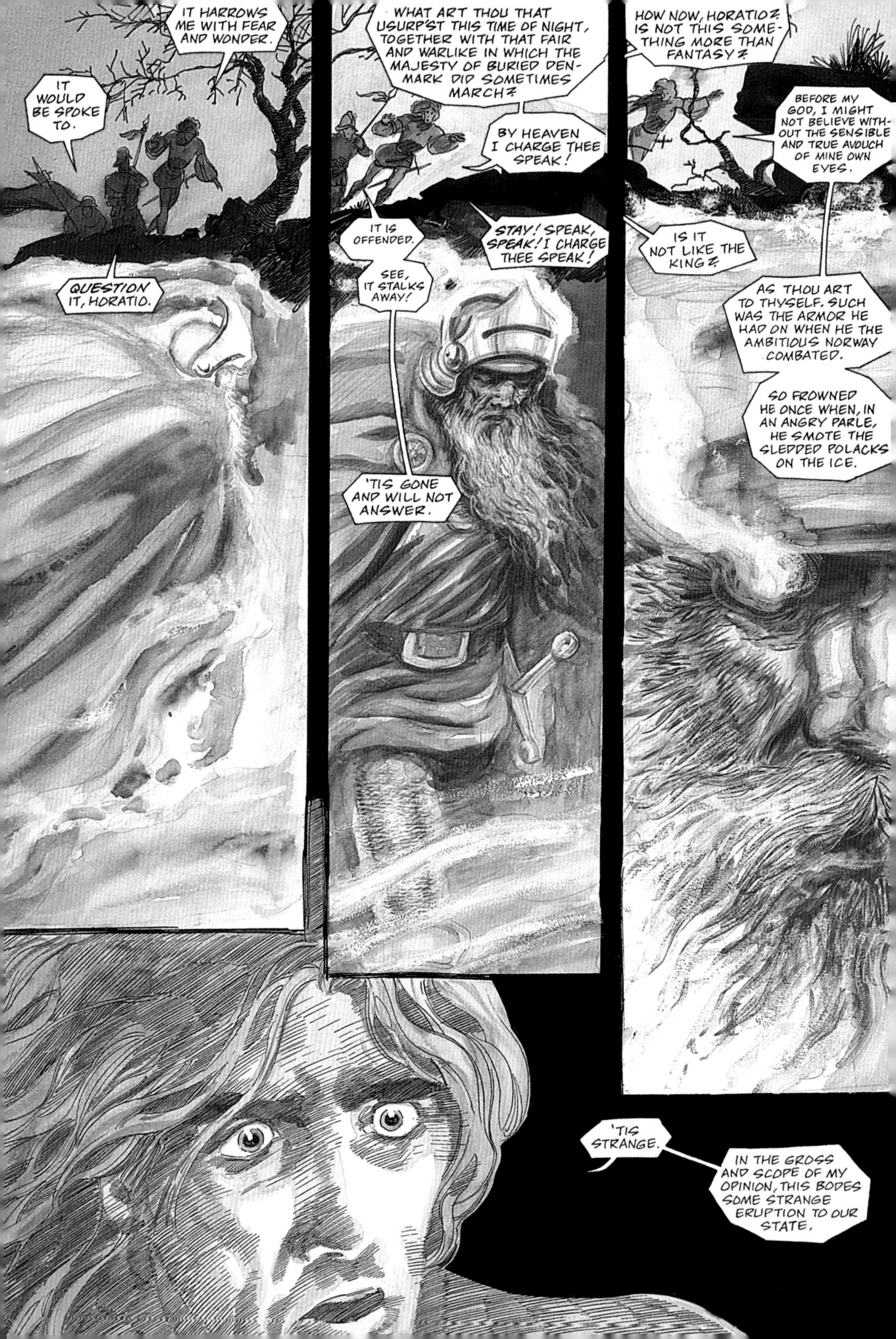
IT HARROWS ME WITH FEAR AND WONDER.
IT WOULD BE SPOKE TO.
QUESTION IT, HORATIO.
WHAT ART THOU THAT USURP'ST THIS TIME OF NIGHT, TOGETHER WITH THAT FAIR AND WARLIKE IN WHICH THE MAJESTY OF BURIED DENMARK DID SOMETIMES MARCH?
BY HEAVEN I CHARGE THEE SPEAK!
IT IS OFFENDED.
STAY! SPEAK, SPEAK! I CHARGE THEE SPEAK!
SEE, IT STALKS AWAY!
'TIS GONE AND WILL NOT ANSWER.
HOW NOW, HORATIO? IS NOT THIS SOMETHING MORE THAN FANTASY?
BEFORE MY GOD, I MIGHT NOT BELIEVE WITHOUT THE SENSIBLE AND TRUE AVOUCH OF MINE OWN EYES.
IS IT NOT LIKE THE KING?
AS THOU ART TO THYSELF. SUCH WAS THE ARMOR HE HAD ON WHEN HE THE AMBITIOUS NORWAY COMBATED.
SO FROWNED HE ONCE WHEN, IN AN ANGRY PARLE, HE SMOTE THE SLEDDED POLACKS ON THE ICE.
'TIS STRANGE.
IN THE GROSS AND SCOPE OF MY OPINION, THIS BODES SOME STRANGE ERUPTION TO OUR STATE.

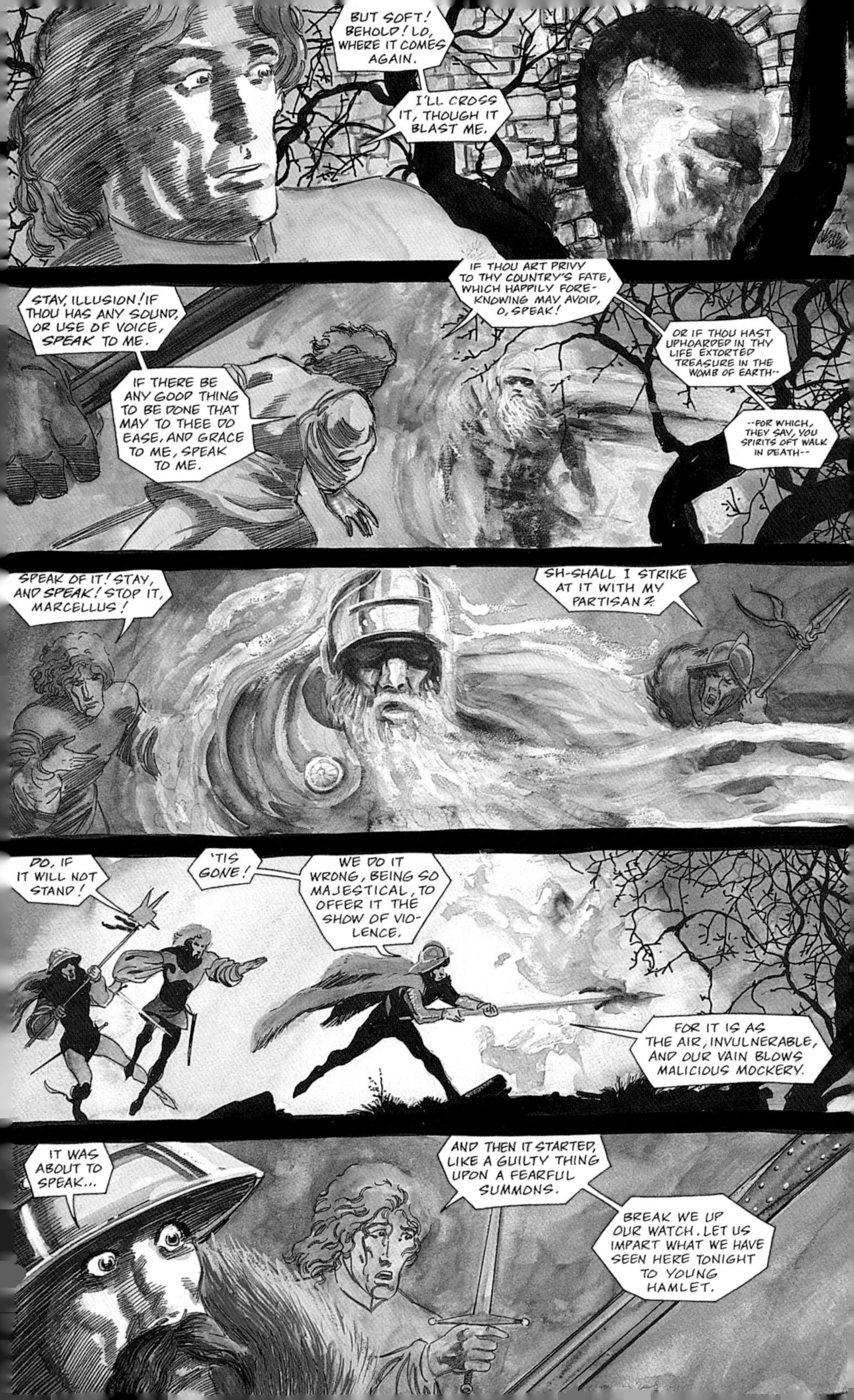
BUT SOFT! BEHOLD! LO, WHERE IT COMES AGAIN.
I'LL CROSS IT, THOUGH IT BLAST ME.
STAY, ILLUSION! IF THOU HAS ANY SOUND, OR USE OF VOICE, SPEAK TO ME.
IF THERE BE ANY GOOD THING TO BE DONE THAT MAY TO THEE DO EASE, AND GRACE TO ME, SPEAK TO ME.
IF THOU ART PRIVY TO THY COUNTRY'S FATE, WHICH HAPPILY FORE-KNOWING MAY AVOID, O, SPEAK!
OR IF THOU HAST UPHOARDED IN THY LIFE EXTORTED TREASURE IN THE WOMB OF EARTH--
--FOR WHICH, THEY SAY, YOU SPIRITS OFT WALK IN DEATH--
SPEAK OF IT! STAY, AND SPEAK! STOP IT, MARCELLUS!
SH-SHALL I STRIKE AT IT WITH MY PARTISAN?
DO, IF IT WILL NOT STAND!
'TIS GONE!
WE DO IT WRONG, BEING SO MAJESTICAL, TO OFFER IT THE SHOW OF VIO-LENCE.
FOR IT IS AS THE AIR, INVULNERABLE, AND OUR VAIN BLOWS MALICIOUS MOCKERY.
IT WAS ABOUT TO SPEAK...
AND THEN IT STARTED, LIKE A GUILTY THING UPON A FEARFUL SUMMONS.
BREAK WE UP OUR WATCH. LET US IMPART WHAT WE HAVE SEEN HERE TONIGHT TO YOUNG HAMLET.

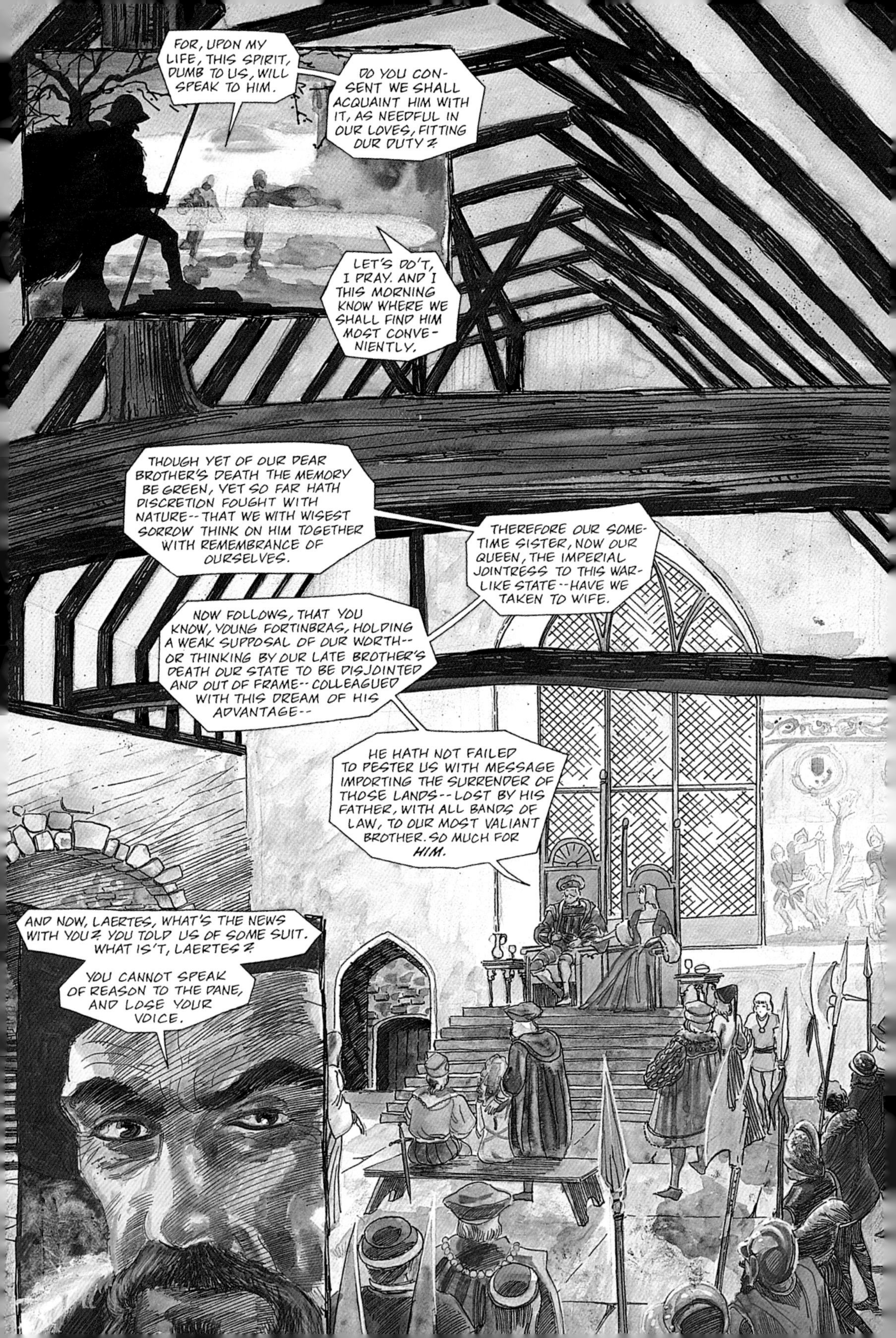

FOR, UPON MY LIFE, THIS SPIRIT, DUMB TO US, WILL SPEAK TO HIM.
DO YOU CONSENT WE SHALL ACQUAINT HIM WITH IT, AS NEEDFUL IN OUR LOVES, FITTING OUR DUTY?
LET'S DO'T, I PRAY. AND I THIS MORNING KNOW WHERE WE SHALL FIND HIM MOST CONVENIENTLY.
THOUGH YET OF OUR DEAR BROTHER'S DEATH THE MEMORY BE GREEN, YET SO FAR HATH DISCRETION FOUGHT WITH NATURE-- THAT WE WITH WISEST SORROW THINK ON HIM TOGETHER WITH REMEMBRANCE OF OURSELVES.
THEREFORE OUR SOMETIME SISTER, NOW OUR QUEEN, THE IMPERIAL JOINTRESS TO THIS WARLIKE STATE--HAVE WE TAKEN TO WIFE.
NOW FOLLOWS, THAT YOU KNOW, YOUNG FORTINBRAS, HOLDING A WEAK SUPPOSAL OF OUR WORTH-- OR THINKING BY OUR LATE BROTHER'S DEATH OUR STATE TO BE DISJOINTED AND OUT OF FRAME-- COLLEAGUED WITH THIS DREAM OF HIS ADVANTAGE--
HE HATH NOT FAILED TO PESTER US WITH MESSAGE IMPORTING THE SURRENDER OF THOSE LANDS--LOST BY HIS FATHER, WITH ALL BANDS OF LAW, TO OUR MOST VALIANT BROTHER. SO MUCH FOR *HIM*.
AND NOW, LAERTES, WHAT'S THE NEWS WITH YOU? YOU TOLD US OF SOME SUIT. WHAT IS'T, LAERTES?
YOU CANNOT SPEAK OF REASON TO THE DANE, AND LOSE YOUR VOICE.

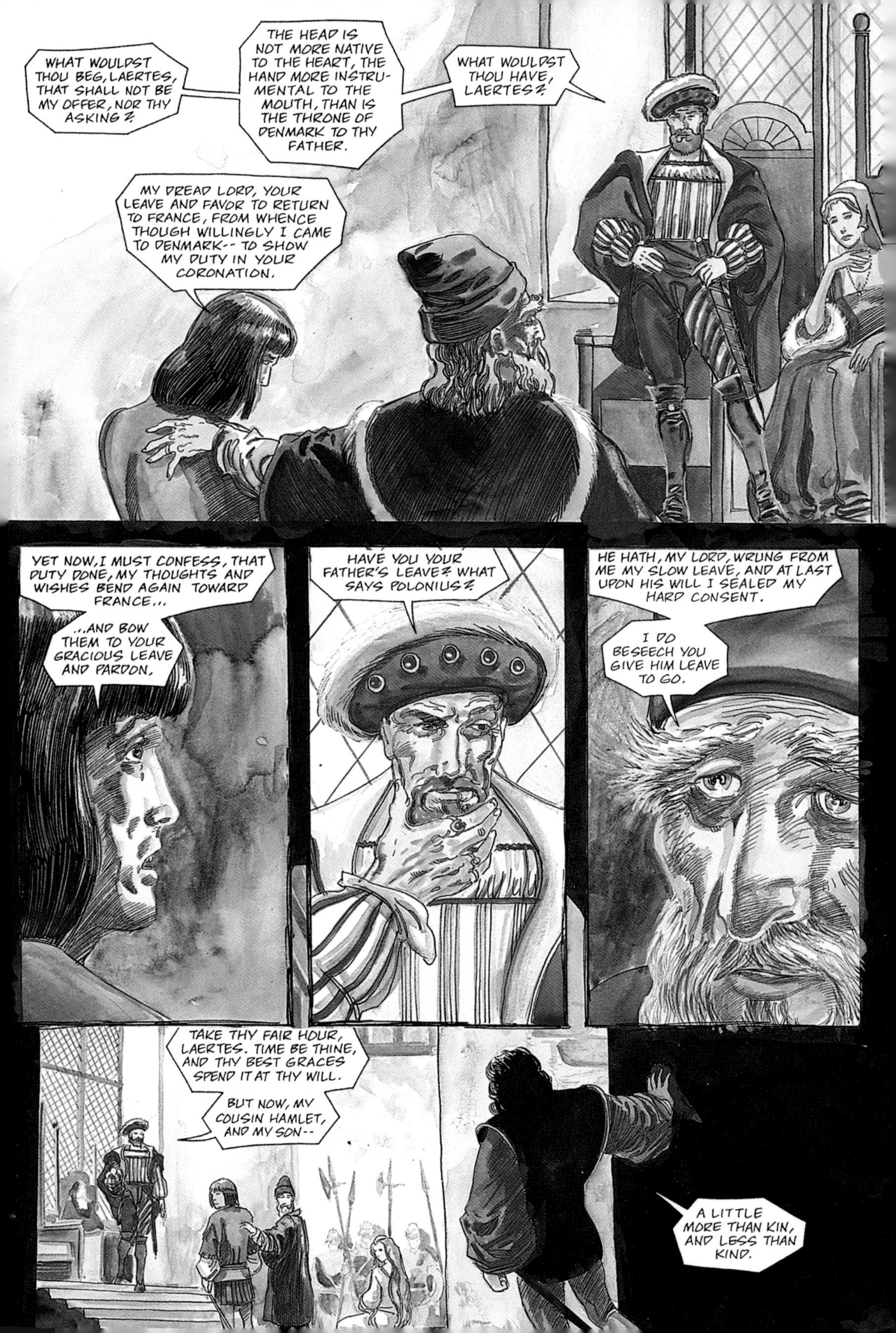
WHAT WOULDST THOU HAVE, LAERTES?
WHAT WOULDST THOU BEG, LAERTES, THAT SHALL NOT BE MY OFFER, NOR THY ASKING?
THE HEAD IS NOT MORE NATIVE TO THE HEART, THE HAND MORE INSTRUMENTAL TO THE MOUTH, THAN IS THE THRONE OF DENMARK TO THY FATHER.
MY DREAD LORD, YOUR LEAVE AND FAVOR TO RETURN TO FRANCE, FROM WHENCE THOUGH WILLINGLY I CAME TO DENMARK-- TO SHOW MY DUTY IN YOUR CORONATION.
YET NOW, I MUST CONFESS, THAT DUTY DONE, MY THOUGHTS AND WISHES BEND AGAIN TOWARD FRANCE...
...AND BOW THEM TO YOUR GRACIOUS LEAVE AND PARDON.
HAVE YOU YOUR FATHER'S LEAVE? WHAT SAYS POLONIUS?
HE HATH, MY LORD, WRUNG FROM ME MY SLOW LEAVE, AND AT LAST UPON HIS WILL I SEALED MY HARD CONSENT.
I DO BESEECH YOU GIVE HIM LEAVE TO GO.
TAKE THY FAIR HOUR, LAERTES. TIME BE THINE, AND THY BEST GRACES SPEND IT AT THY WILL.
BUT NOW, MY COUSIN HAMLET, AND MY SON--
A LITTLE MORE THAN KIN, AND LESS THAN KIND.

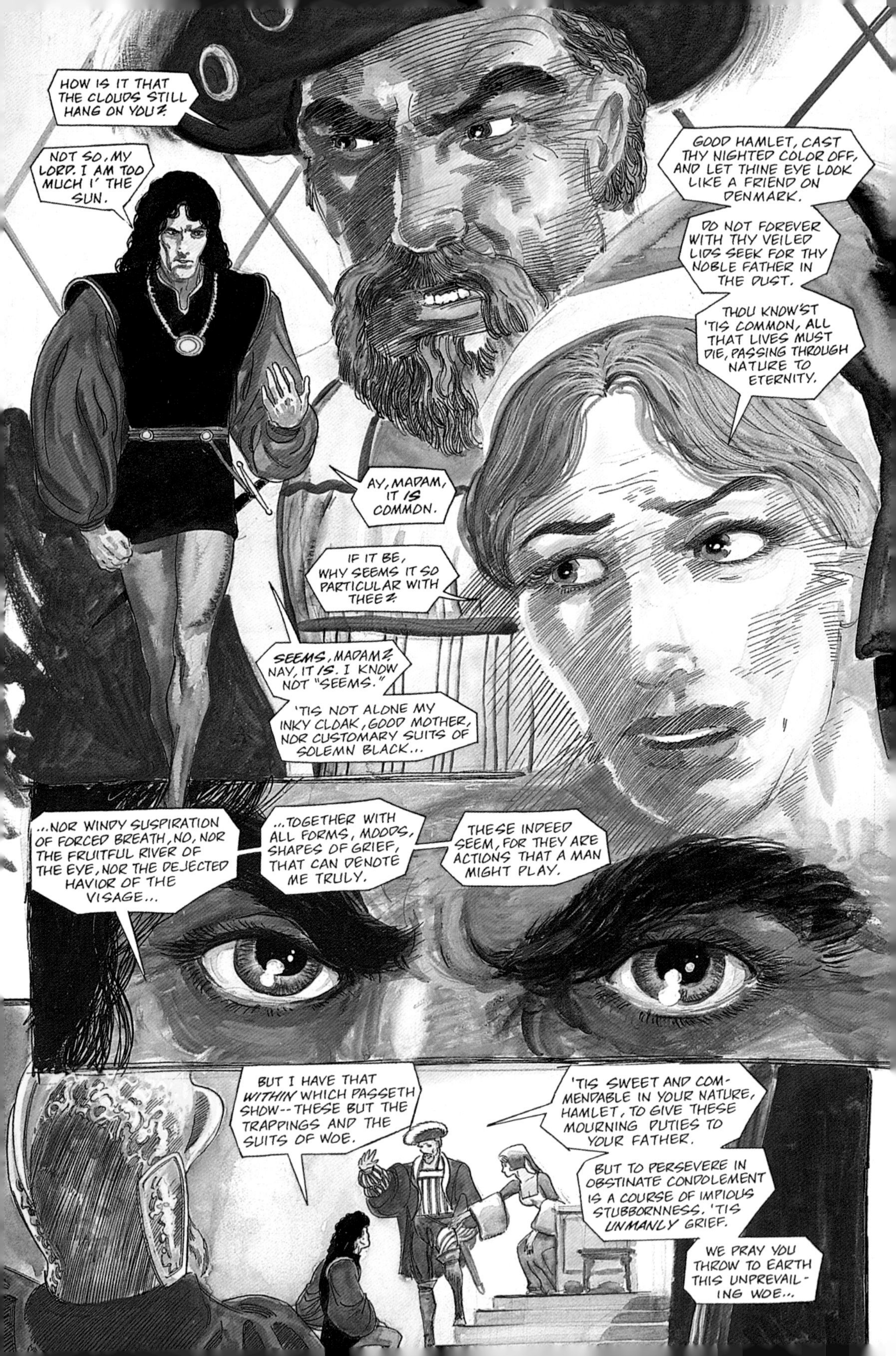
HOW IS IT THAT THE CLOUDS STILL HANG ON YOU?
NOT SO, MY LORD. I AM TOO MUCH I' THE SUN.
GOOD HAMLET, CAST THY NIGHTED COLOR OFF, AND LET THINE EYE LOOK LIKE A FRIEND ON DENMARK.
DO NOT FOREVER WITH THY VEILED LIDS SEEK FOR THY NOBLE FATHER IN THE DUST.
THOU KNOW'ST 'TIS COMMON, ALL THAT LIVES MUST DIE, PASSING THROUGH NATURE TO ETERNITY.
AY, MADAM, IT IS COMMON.
IF IT BE, WHY SEEMS IT SO PARTICULAR WITH THEE?
SEEMS, MADAM? NAY, IT IS. I KNOW NOT "SEEMS."
'TIS NOT ALONE MY INKY CLOAK, GOOD MOTHER, NOR CUSTOMARY SUITS OF SOLEMN BLACK...
...NOR WINDY SUSPIRATION OF FORCED BREATH, NO, NOR THE FRUITFUL RIVER OF THE EYE, NOR THE DEJECTED HAVIOR OF THE VISAGE...
...TOGETHER WITH ALL FORMS, MOODS, SHAPES OF GRIEF, THAT CAN DENOTE ME TRULY.
THESE INDEED SEEM, FOR THEY ARE ACTIONS THAT A MAN MIGHT PLAY.
BUT I HAVE THAT WITHIN WHICH PASSETH SHOW--THESE BUT THE TRAPPINGS AND THE SUITS OF WOE.
'TIS SWEET AND COMMENDABLE IN YOUR NATURE, HAMLET, TO GIVE THESE MOURNING DUTIES TO YOUR FATHER.
BUT TO PERSEVERE IN OBSTINATE CONDOLEMENT IS A COURSE OF IMPIOUS STUBBORNNESS. 'TIS UNMANLY GRIEF.
WE PRAY YOU THROW TO EARTH THIS UNPREVAILING WOE...

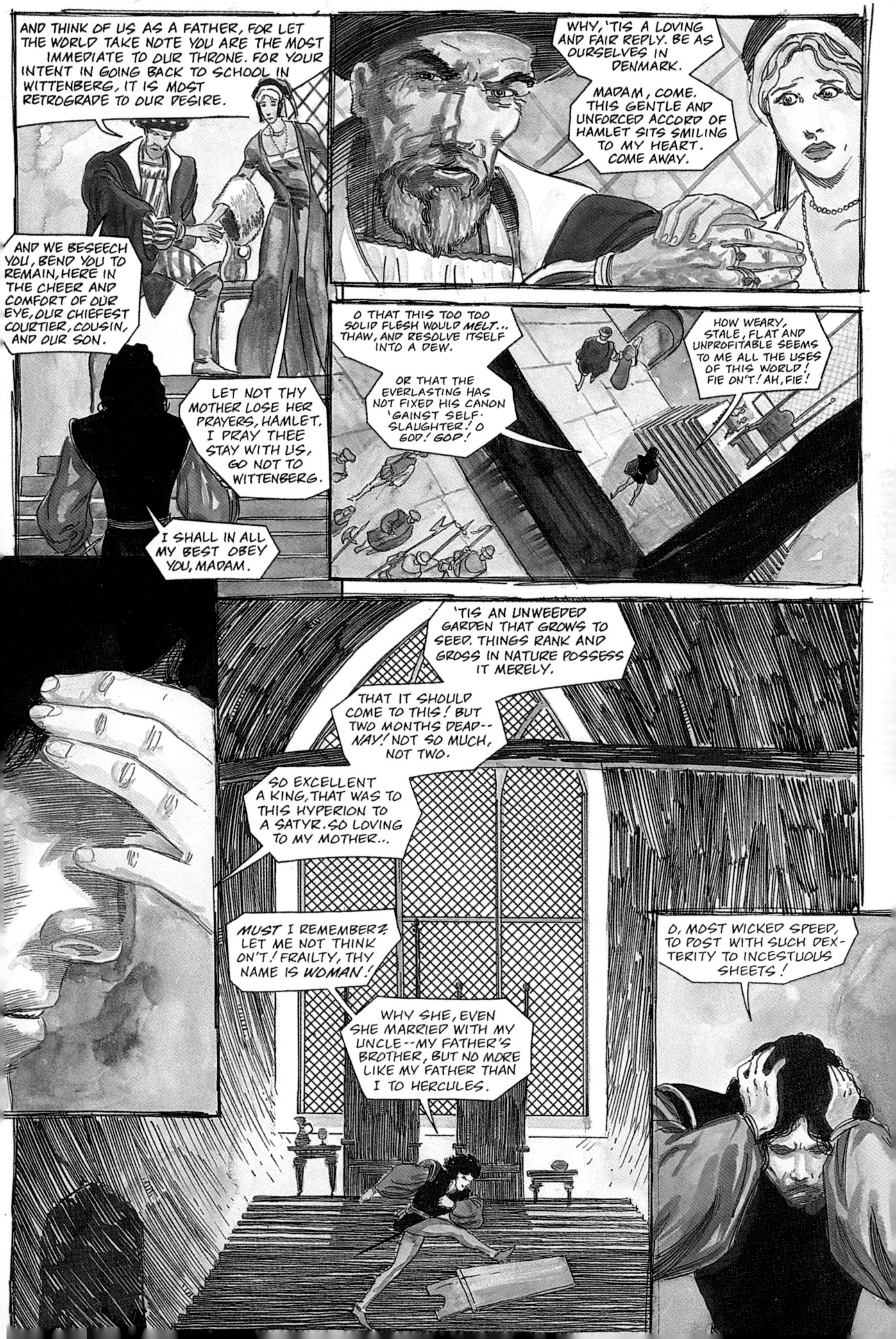
AND THINK OF US AS A FATHER, FOR LET THE WORLD TAKE NOTE YOU ARE THE MOST IMMEDIATE TO OUR THRONE. FOR YOUR INTENT IN GOING BACK TO SCHOOL IN WITTENBERG, IT IS MOST RETROGRADE TO OUR DESIRE.
AND WE BESEECH YOU, BEND YOU TO REMAIN, HERE IN THE CHEER AND COMFORT OF OUR EYE, OUR CHIEFEST COURTIER, COUSIN, AND OUR SON.
LET NOT THY MOTHER LOSE HER PRAYERS, HAMLET. I PRAY THEE STAY WITH US, GO NOT TO WITTENBERG.
I SHALL IN ALL MY BEST OBEY YOU, MADAM.
WHY, 'TIS A LOVING AND FAIR REPLY. BE AS OURSELVES IN DENMARK.
MADAM, COME. THIS GENTLE AND UNFORCED ACCORD OF HAMLET SITS SMILING TO MY HEART. COME AWAY.
O THAT THIS TOO TOO SOLID FLESH WOULD MELT... THAW, AND RESOLVE ITSELF INTO A DEW.
OR THAT THE EVERLASTING HAS NOT FIXED HIS CANON 'GAINST SELF-SLAUGHTER! O GOD! GOD!
HOW WEARY, STALE, FLAT AND UNPROFITABLE SEEMS TO ME ALL THE USES OF THIS WORLD! FIE ON'T! AH, FIE!
'TIS AN UNWEEDED GARDEN THAT GROWS TO SEED. THINGS RANK AND GROSS IN NATURE POSSESS IT MERELY.
THAT IT SHOULD COME TO THIS! BUT TWO MONTHS DEAD-- NAY! NOT SO MUCH, NOT TWO.
SO EXCELLENT A KING, THAT WAS TO THIS HYPERION TO A SATYR. SO LOVING TO MY MOTHER...
MUST I REMEMBER? LET ME NOT THINK ON'T! FRAILTY, THY NAME IS WOMAN!
WHY SHE, EVEN SHE MARRIED WITH MY UNCLE--MY FATHER'S BROTHER, BUT NO MORE LIKE MY FATHER THAN I TO HERCULES.
O, MOST WICKED SPEED, TO POST WITH SUCH DEXTERITY TO INCESTUOUS SHEETS!

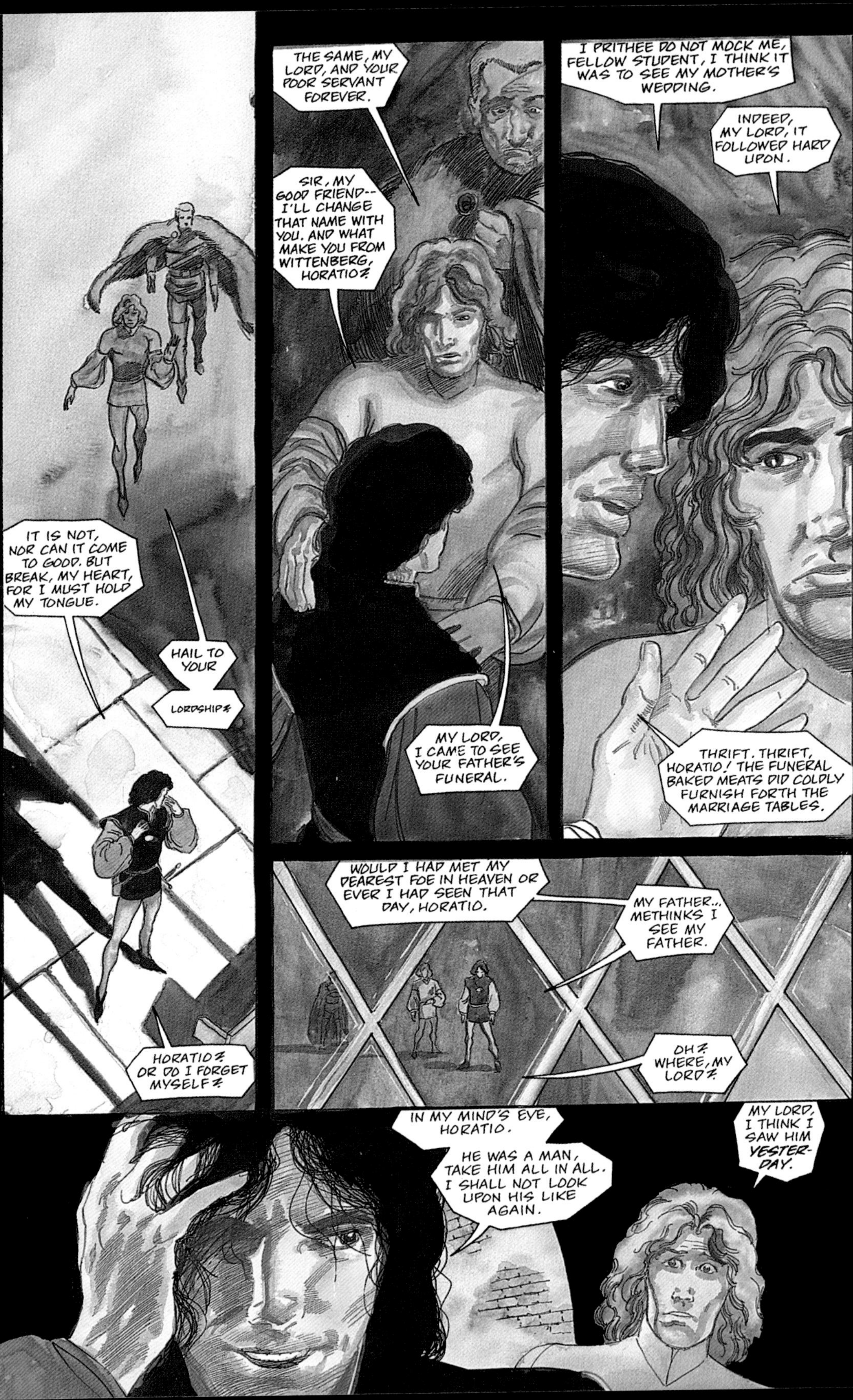
IT IS NOT, NOR CAN IT COME TO GOOD. BUT BREAK, MY HEART, FOR I MUST HOLD MY TONGUE.
HAIL TO YOUR
LORDSHIP!
HORATIO! OR DO I FORGET MYSELF!
THE SAME, MY LORD, AND YOUR POOR SERVANT FOREVER.
SIR, MY GOOD FRIEND-- I'LL CHANGE THAT NAME WITH YOU. AND WHAT MAKE YOU FROM WITTENBERG, HORATIO?
MY LORD, I CAME TO SEE YOUR FATHER'S FUNERAL.
I PRITHEE DO NOT MOCK ME, FELLOW STUDENT, I THINK IT WAS TO SEE MY MOTHER'S WEDDING.
INDEED, MY LORD, IT FOLLOWED HARD UPON.
THRIFT. THRIFT, HORATIO! THE FUNERAL BAKED MEATS DID COLDLY FURNISH FORTH THE MARRIAGE TABLES.
WOULD I HAD MET MY DEAREST FOE IN HEAVEN OR EVER I HAD SEEN THAT DAY, HORATIO.
MY FATHER... METHINKS I SEE MY FATHER.
OH? WHERE, MY LORD?
IN MY MIND'S EYE, HORATIO.
HE WAS A MAN, TAKE HIM ALL IN ALL. I SHALL NOT LOOK UPON HIS LIKE AGAIN.
MY LORD, I THINK I SAW HIM YESTER-DAY.

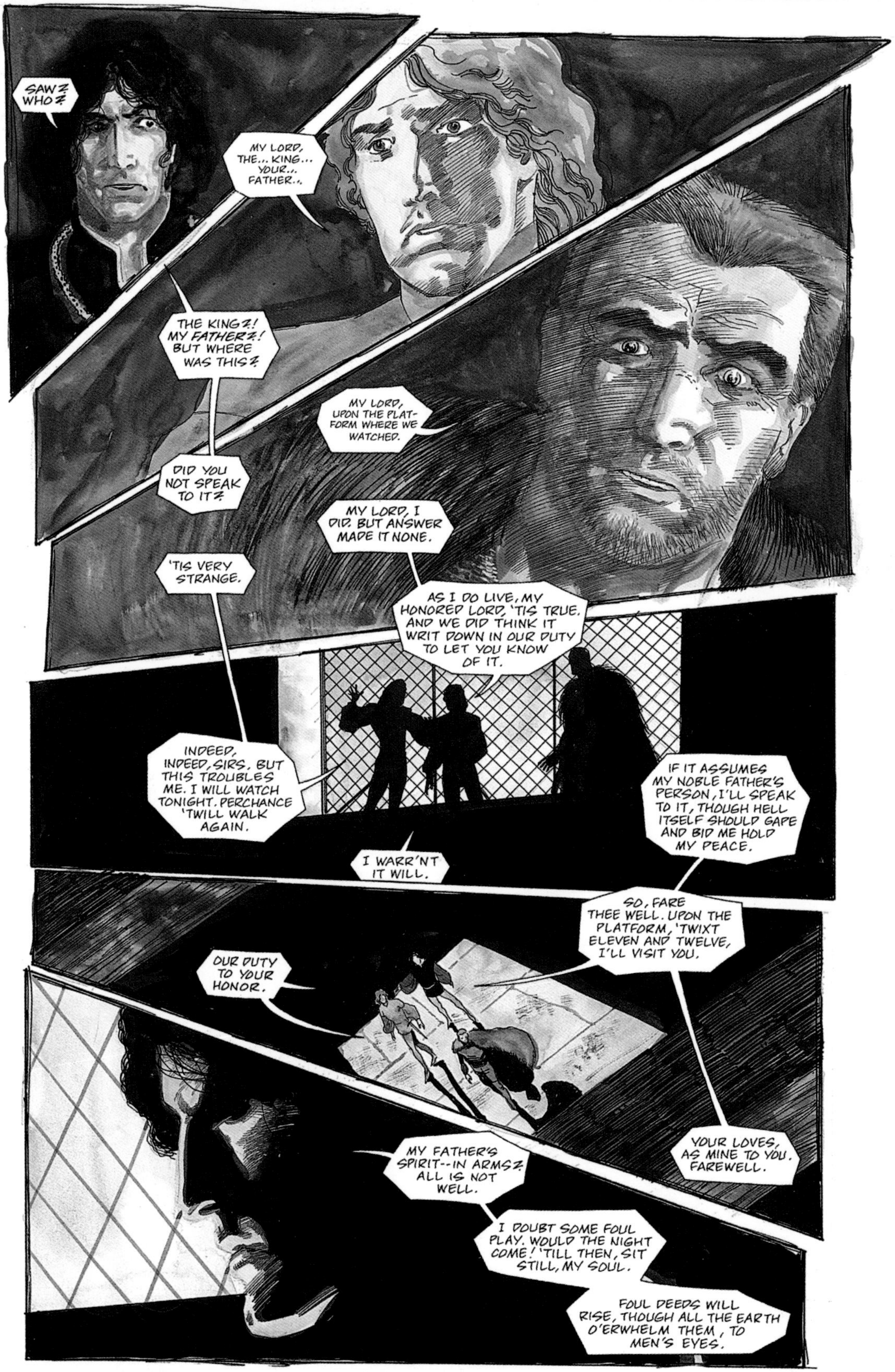
SAW? WHO?
MY LORD, THE... KING... YOUR... FATHER...
THE KING?! MY FATHER?! BUT WHERE WAS THIS?
MY LORD, UPON THE PLATFORM WHERE WE WATCHED.
DID YOU NOT SPEAK TO IT?
MY LORD, I DID. BUT ANSWER MADE IT NONE.
'TIS VERY STRANGE.
AS I DO LIVE, MY HONORED LORD, 'TIS TRUE. AND WE DID THINK IT WRIT DOWN IN OUR DUTY TO LET YOU KNOW OF IT.
INDEED, INDEED, SIRS. BUT THIS TROUBLES ME. I WILL WATCH TONIGHT. PERCHANCE 'TWILL WALK AGAIN.
I WARR'NT IT WILL.
IF IT ASSUMES MY NOBLE FATHER'S PERSON, I'LL SPEAK TO IT, THOUGH HELL ITSELF SHOULD GAPE AND BID ME HOLD MY PEACE.
SO, FARE THEE WELL. UPON THE PLATFORM, 'TWIXT ELEVEN AND TWELVE, I'LL VISIT YOU.
OUR DUTY TO YOUR HONOR.
YOUR LOVES, AS MINE TO YOU. FAREWELL.
MY FATHER'S SPIRIT--IN ARMS? ALL IS NOT WELL.
I DOUBT SOME FOUL PLAY. WOULD THE NIGHT COME! 'TILL THEN, SIT STILL, MY SOUL.
FOUL DEEDS WILL RISE, THOUGH ALL THE EARTH O'ERWHELM THEM, TO MEN'S EYES.

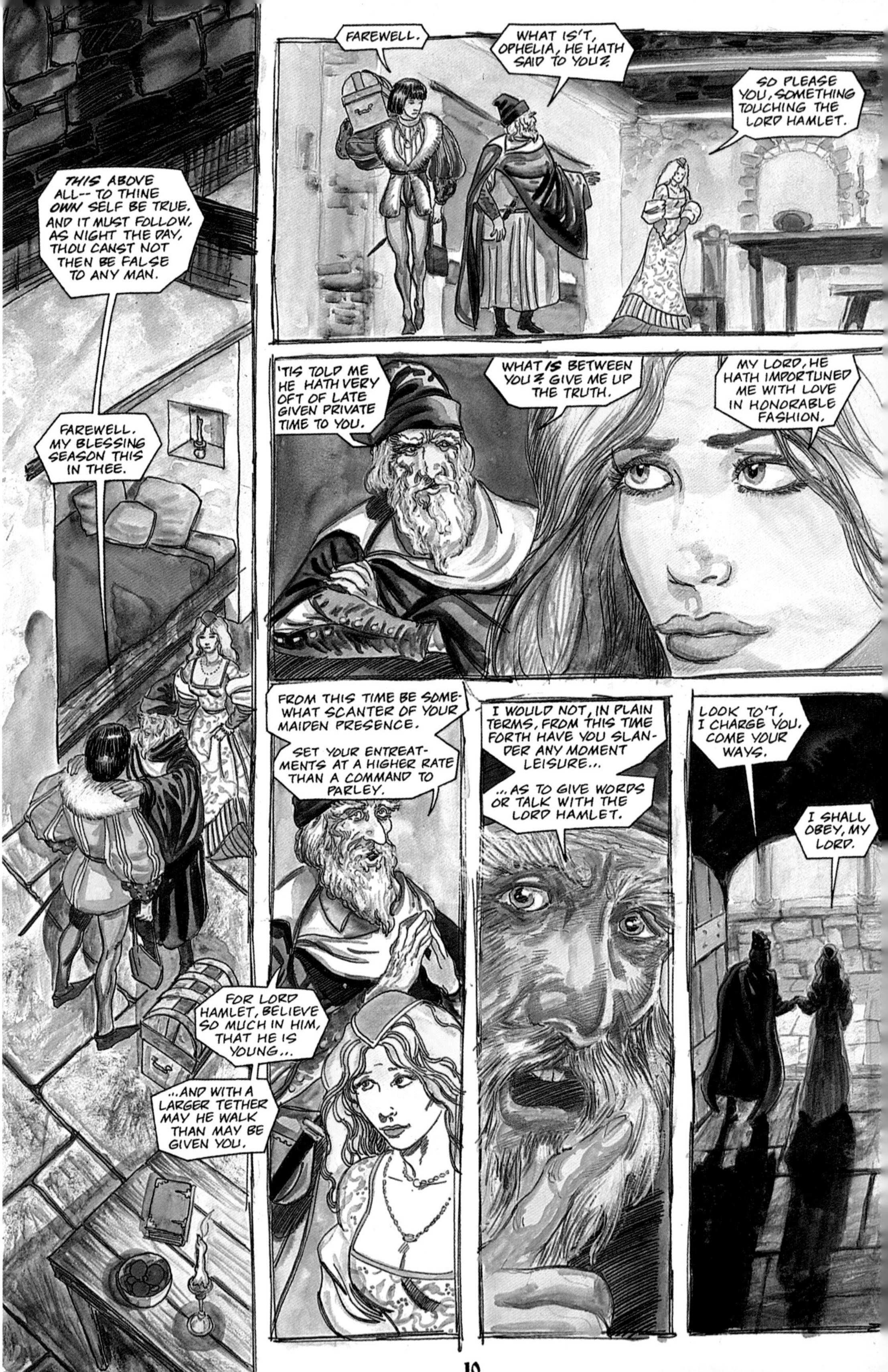
THIS ABOVE ALL-- TO THINE OWN SELF BE TRUE, AND IT MUST FOLLOW, AS NIGHT THE DAY, THOU CANST NOT THEN BE FALSE TO ANY MAN.
FAREWELL. MY BLESSING SEASON THIS IN THEE.
FAREWELL.
WHAT IS'T, OPHELIA, HE HATH SAID TO YOU?
SO PLEASE YOU, SOMETHING TOUCHING THE LORD HAMLET.
'TIS TOLD ME HE HATH VERY OFT OF LATE GIVEN PRIVATE TIME TO YOU.
WHAT IS BETWEEN YOU? GIVE ME UP THE TRUTH.
MY LORD, HE HATH IMPORTUNED ME WITH LOVE IN HONORABLE FASHION.
FROM THIS TIME BE SOMEWHAT SCANTER OF YOUR MAIDEN PRESENCE.
SET YOUR ENTREATMENTS AT A HIGHER RATE THAN A COMMAND TO PARLEY.
FOR LORD HAMLET, BELIEVE SO MUCH IN HIM, THAT HE IS YOUNG...
...AND WITH A LARGER TETHER MAY HE WALK THAN MAY BE GIVEN YOU.
I WOULD NOT, IN PLAIN TERMS, FROM THIS TIME FORTH HAVE YOU SLANDER ANY MOMENT LEISURE...
...AS TO GIVE WORDS OR TALK WITH THE LORD HAMLET.
LOOK TO'T, I CHARGE YOU. COME YOUR WAYS.
I SHALL OBEY, MY LORD.

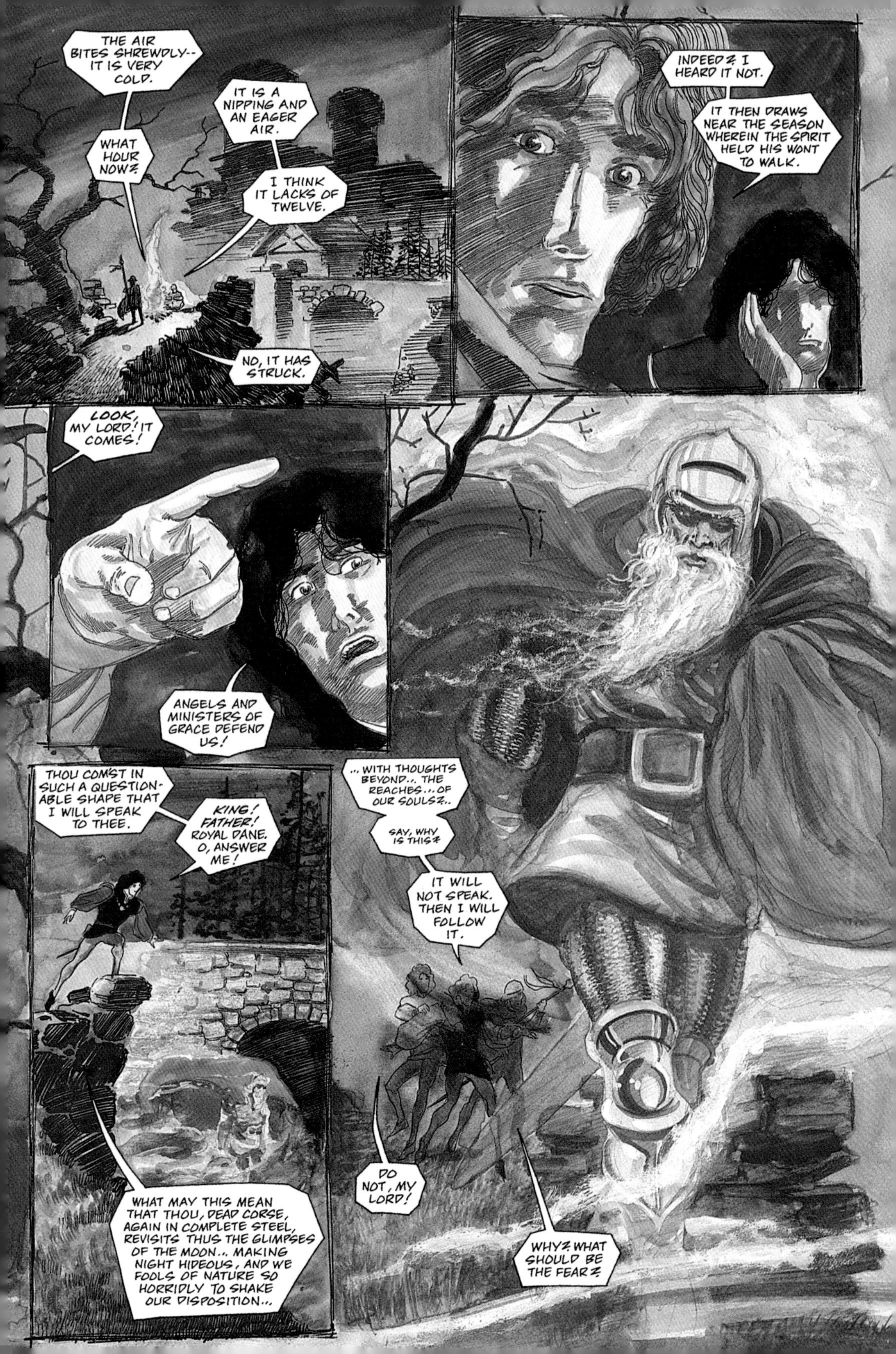
THE AIR BITES SHREWDLY-- IT IS VERY COLD.
WHAT HOUR NOW?
IT IS A NIPPING AND AN EAGER AIR.
I THINK IT LACKS OF TWELVE.
NO, IT HAS STRUCK.
INDEED? I HEARD IT NOT.
IT THEN DRAWS NEAR THE SEASON WHEREIN THE SPIRIT HELD HIS WONT TO WALK.
LOOK, MY LORD! IT *COMES!*
ANGELS AND MINISTERS OF GRACE DEFEND US!
THOU COM'ST IN SUCH A QUESTIONABLE SHAPE THAT I WILL SPEAK TO THEE.
KING! FATHER! ROYAL DANE. O, ANSWER ME!
WHAT MAY THIS MEAN THAT THOU, DEAD CORSE, AGAIN IN COMPLETE STEEL, REVISITS THUS THE GLIMPSES OF THE MOON... MAKING NIGHT HIDEOUS, AND WE FOOLS OF NATURE SO HORRIDLY TO SHAKE OUR DISPOSITION...
...WITH THOUGHTS BEYOND... THE REACHES... OF OUR SOULS?..
SAY, WHY IS THIS?
IT WILL NOT SPEAK. THEN I WILL FOLLOW IT.
DO NOT, MY LORD!
WHY? WHAT SHOULD BE THE FEAR?

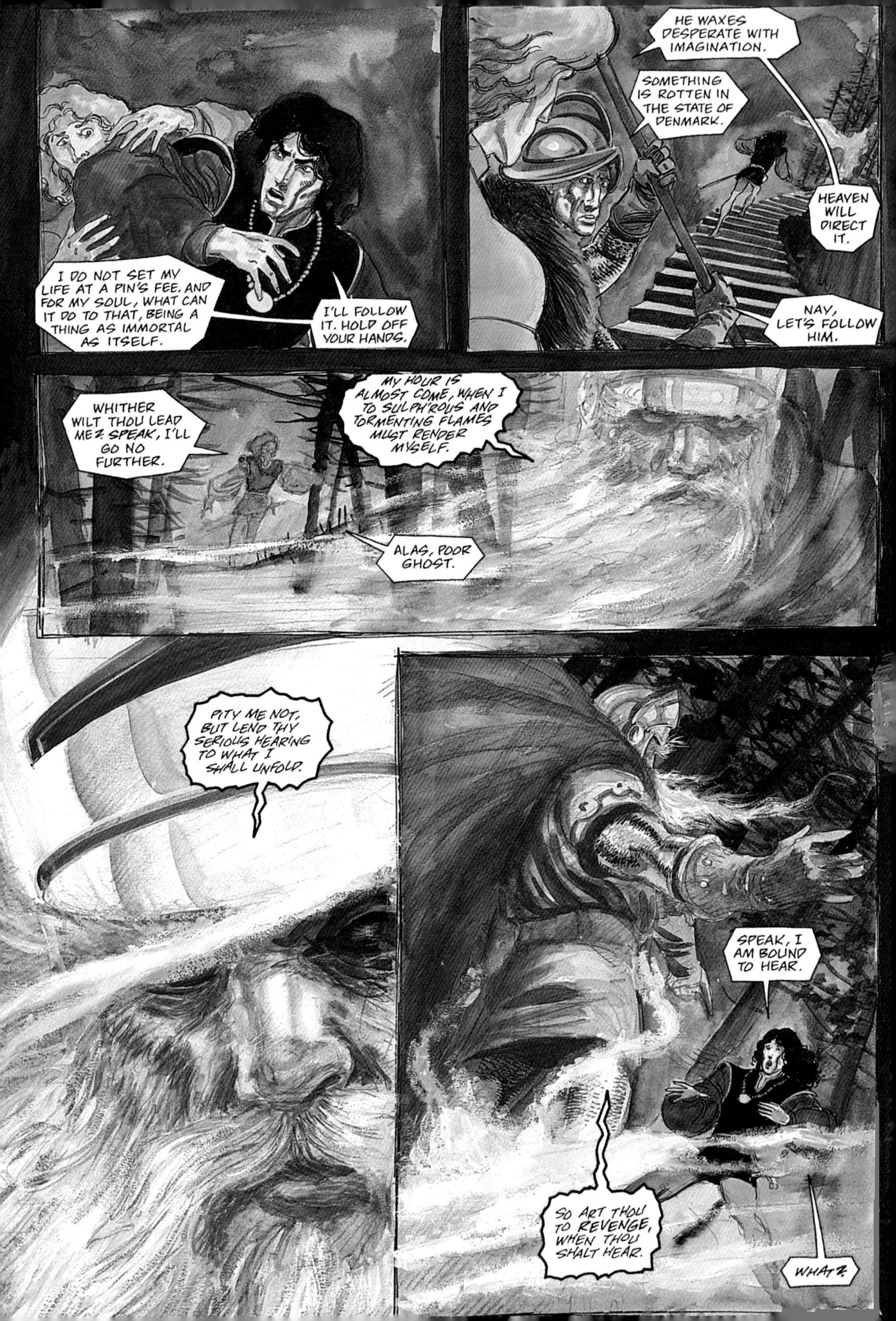
I DO NOT SET MY LIFE AT A PIN'S FEE. AND FOR MY SOUL, WHAT CAN IT DO TO THAT, BEING A THING AS IMMORTAL AS ITSELF.
I'LL FOLLOW IT. HOLD OFF YOUR HANDS.
HE WAXES DESPERATE WITH IMAGINATION.
SOMETHING IS ROTTEN IN THE STATE OF DENMARK.
HEAVEN WILL DIRECT IT.
NAY, LET'S FOLLOW HIM.
WHITHER WILT THOU LEAD ME? SPEAK, I'LL GO NO FURTHER.
MY HOUR IS ALMOST COME, WHEN I TO SULPH'ROUS AND TORMENTING FLAMES MUST RENDER MYSELF.
ALAS, POOR GHOST.
PITY ME NOT, BUT LEND THY SERIOUS HEARING TO WHAT I SHALL UNFOLD.
SPEAK, I AM BOUND TO HEAR.
SO ART THOU TO REVENGE, WHEN THOU SHALT HEAR.
WHAT?

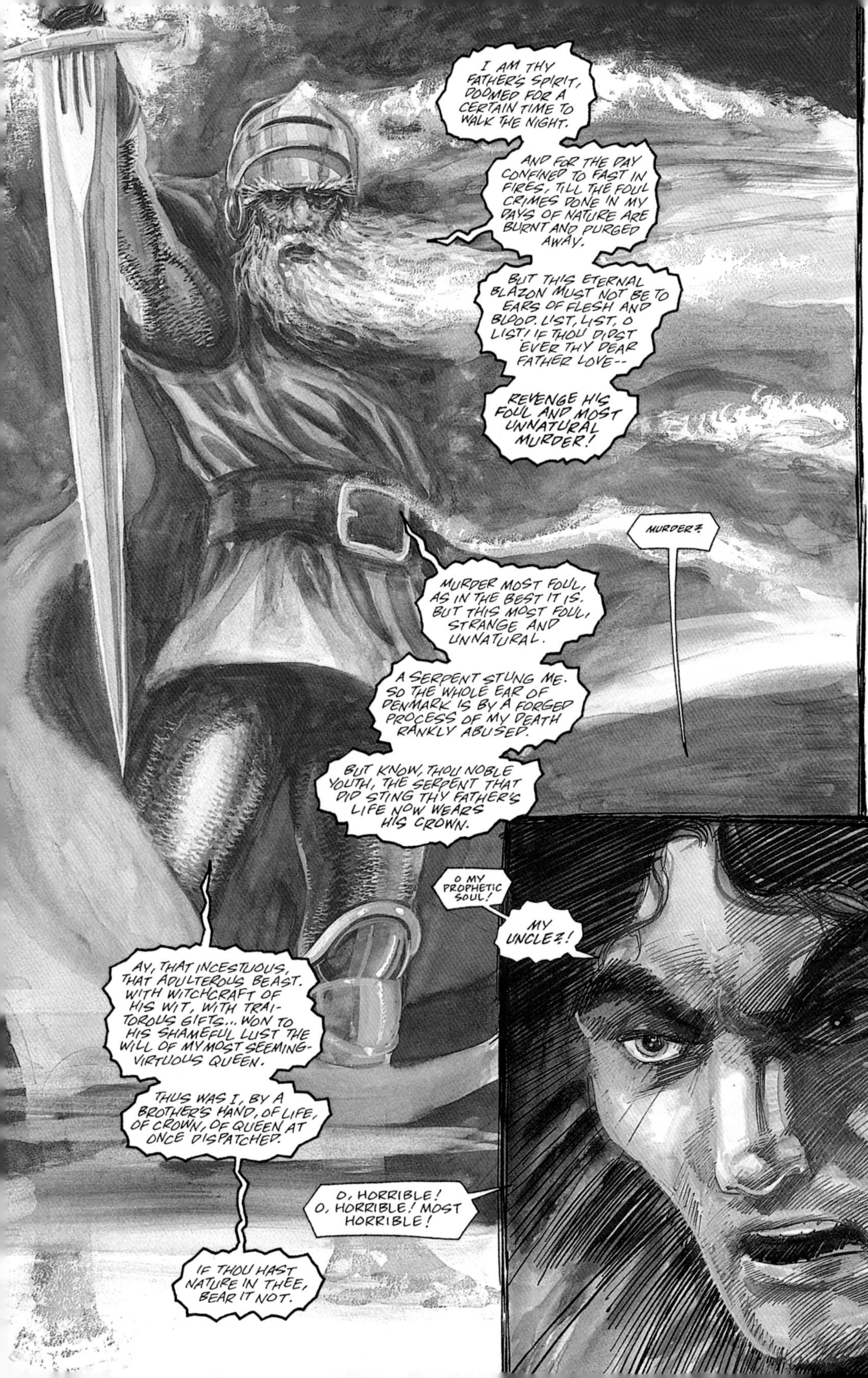
I AM THY FATHER'S SPIRIT, DOOMED FOR A CERTAIN TIME TO WALK THE NIGHT.
AND FOR THE DAY CONFINED TO FAST IN FIRES, TILL THE FOUL CRIMES DONE IN MY DAYS OF NATURE ARE BURNT AND PURGED AWAY.
BUT THIS ETERNAL BLAZON MUST NOT BE TO EARS OF FLESH AND BLOOD. LIST, LIST, O LIST! IF THOU DIDST EVER THY DEAR FATHER LOVE--
REVENGE HIS FOUL AND MOST UNNATURAL MURDER!
MURDER?
MURDER MOST FOUL, AS IN THE BEST IT IS. BUT THIS MOST FOUL, STRANGE AND UNNATURAL.
A SERPENT STUNG ME. SO THE WHOLE EAR OF DENMARK IS BY A FORGED PROCESS OF MY DEATH RANKLY ABUSED.
BUT KNOW, THOU NOBLE YOUTH, THE SERPENT THAT DID STING THY FATHER'S LIFE NOW WEARS HIS CROWN.
O MY PROPHETIC SOUL!
MY UNCLE?!
AY, THAT INCESTUOUS, THAT ADULTEROUS BEAST. WITH WITCHCRAFT OF HIS WIT, WITH TRAITOROUS GIFTS... WON TO HIS SHAMEFUL LUST THE WILL OF MY MOST SEEMING-VIRTUOUS QUEEN.
THUS WAS I, BY A BROTHER'S HAND, OF LIFE, OF CROWN, OF QUEEN AT ONCE DISPATCHED.
O, HORRIBLE! O, HORRIBLE! MOST HORRIBLE!
IF THOU HAST NATURE IN THEE, BEAR IT NOT.

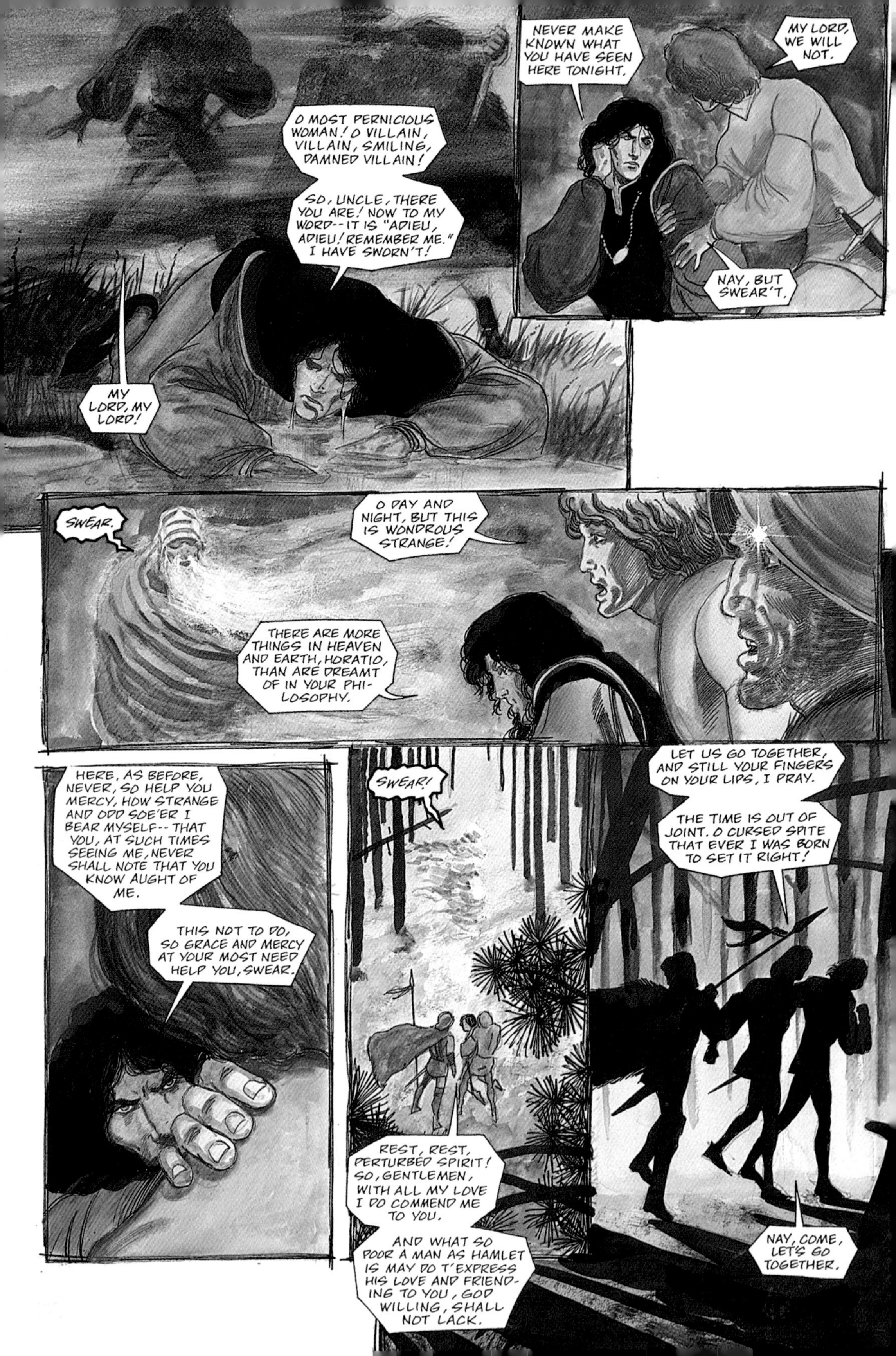
O MOST PERNICIOUS WOMAN! O VILLAIN, VILLAIN, SMILING, DAMNED VILLAIN!
SO, UNCLE, THERE YOU ARE! NOW TO MY WORD--IT IS "ADIEU, ADIEU! REMEMBER ME." I HAVE SWORN'T!
MY LORD, MY LORD!
NEVER MAKE KNOWN WHAT YOU HAVE SEEN HERE TONIGHT.
MY LORD, WE WILL NOT.
NAY, BUT SWEAR'T.
SWEAR.
O DAY AND NIGHT, BUT THIS IS WONDROUS STRANGE!
THERE ARE MORE THINGS IN HEAVEN AND EARTH, HORATIO, THAN ARE DREAMT OF IN YOUR PHILOSOPHY.
HERE, AS BEFORE, NEVER, SO HELP YOU MERCY, HOW STRANGE AND ODD SOE'ER I BEAR MYSELF-- THAT YOU, AT SUCH TIMES SEEING ME, NEVER SHALL NOTE THAT YOU KNOW AUGHT OF ME.
THIS NOT TO DO, SO GRACE AND MERCY AT YOUR MOST NEED HELP YOU, SWEAR.
SWEAR!
REST, REST, PERTURBED SPIRIT! SO, GENTLEMEN, WITH ALL MY LOVE I DO COMMEND ME TO YOU.
AND WHAT SO POOR A MAN AS HAMLET IS MAY DO T'EXPRESS HIS LOVE AND FRIENDING TO YOU, GOD WILLING, SHALL NOT LACK.
LET US GO TOGETHER, AND STILL YOUR FINGERS ON YOUR LIPS, I PRAY.
THE TIME IS OUT OF JOINT. O CURSED SPITE THAT EVER I WAS BORN TO SET IT RIGHT!
NAY, COME, LET'S GO TOGETHER.

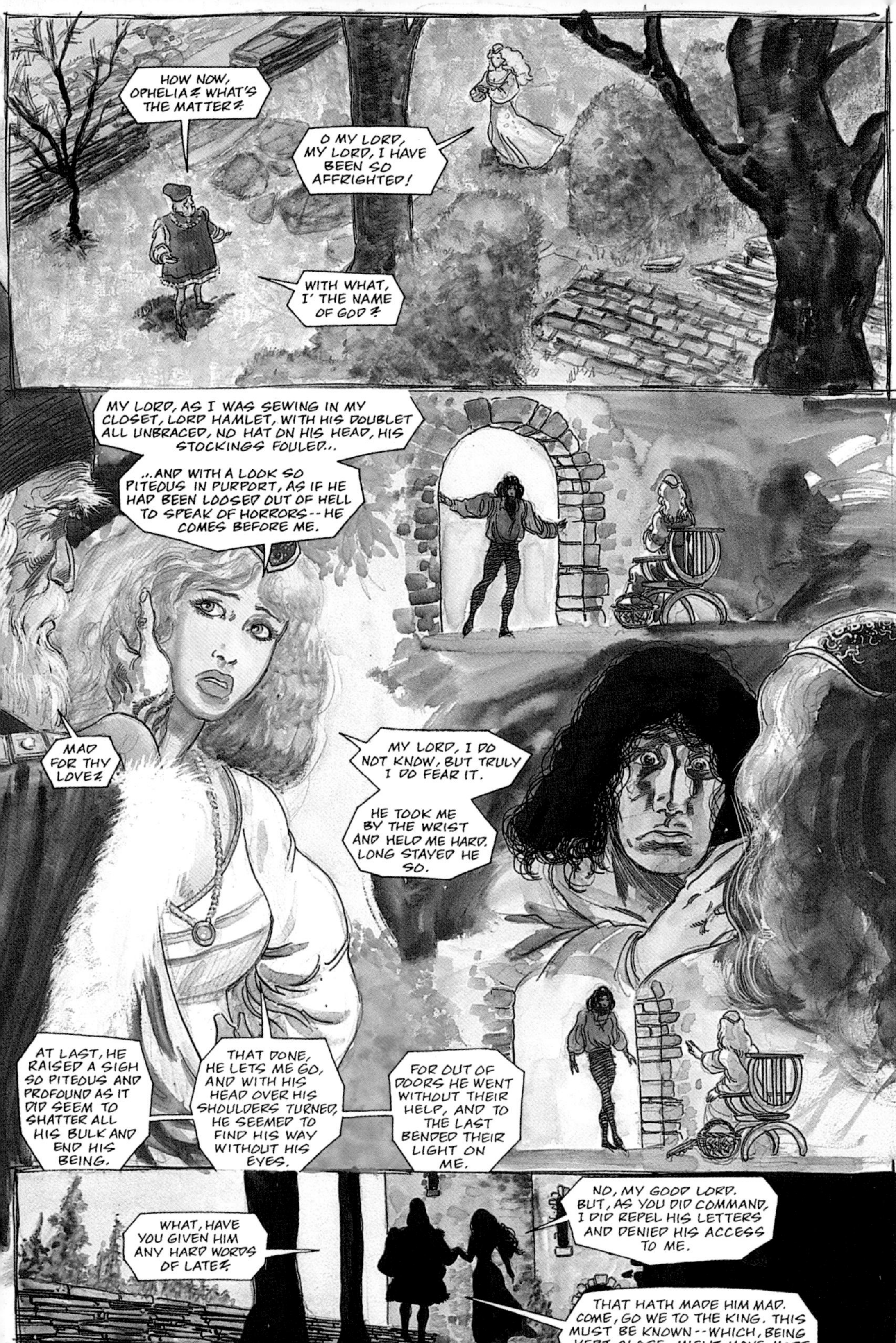
HOW NOW, OPHELIA? WHAT'S THE MATTER?
O MY LORD, MY LORD, I HAVE BEEN SO AFFRIGHTED!
WITH WHAT, I' THE NAME OF GOD?
MY LORD, AS I WAS SEWING IN MY CLOSET, LORD HAMLET, WITH HIS DOUBLET ALL UNBRACED, NO HAT ON HIS HEAD, HIS STOCKINGS FOULED..
..AND WITH A LOOK SO PITEOUS IN PURPORT, AS IF HE HAD BEEN LOOSED OUT OF HELL TO SPEAK OF HORRORS--HE COMES BEFORE ME.
MAD FOR THY LOVE?
MY LORD, I DO NOT KNOW, BUT TRULY I DO FEAR IT.
HE TOOK ME BY THE WRIST AND HELD ME HARD. LONG STAYED HE SO.
AT LAST, HE RAISED A SIGH SO PITEOUS AND PROFOUND AS IT DID SEEM TO SHATTER ALL HIS BULK AND END HIS BEING.
THAT DONE, HE LETS ME GO, AND WITH HIS HEAD OVER HIS SHOULDERS TURNED, HE SEEMED TO FIND HIS WAY WITHOUT HIS EYES.
FOR OUT OF DOORS HE WENT WITHOUT THEIR HELP, AND TO THE LAST BENDED THEIR LIGHT ON ME.
WHAT, HAVE YOU GIVEN HIM ANY HARD WORDS OF LATE?
NO, MY GOOD LORD. BUT, AS YOU DID COMMAND, I DID REPEL HIS LETTERS AND DENIED HIS ACCESS TO ME.
THAT HATH MADE HIM MAD. COME, GO WE TO THE KING. THIS MUST BE KNOWN--WHICH, BEING KEPT CLOSE, MIGHT MOVE MORE GRIEF TO HIDE THAN HATE TO UTTER LOVE. COME.

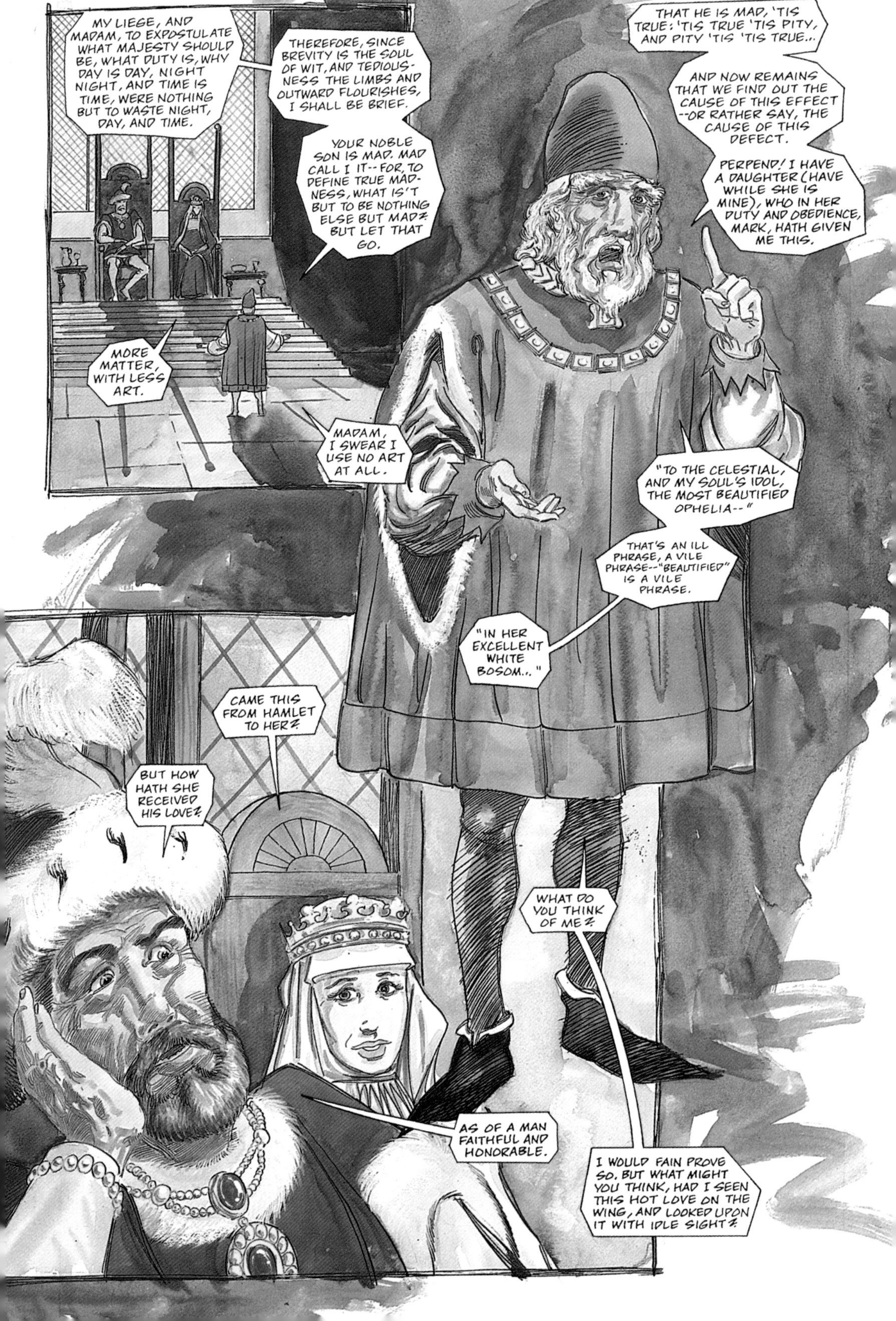
MY LIEGE, AND MADAM, TO EXPOSTULATE WHAT MAJESTY SHOULD BE, WHAT DUTY IS, WHY DAY IS DAY, NIGHT NIGHT, AND TIME IS TIME, WERE NOTHING BUT TO WASTE NIGHT, DAY, AND TIME.
THEREFORE, SINCE BREVITY IS THE SOUL OF WIT, AND TEDIOUSNESS THE LIMBS AND OUTWARD FLOURISHES, I SHALL BE BRIEF.
YOUR NOBLE SON IS MAD. MAD CALL I IT--FOR, TO DEFINE TRUE MADNESS, WHAT IS'T BUT TO BE NOTHING ELSE BUT MAD? BUT LET THAT GO.
MORE MATTER, WITH LESS ART.
MADAM, I SWEAR I USE NO ART AT ALL.
THAT HE IS MAD, 'TIS TRUE: 'TIS TRUE 'TIS PITY, AND PITY 'TIS 'TIS TRUE...
AND NOW REMAINS THAT WE FIND OUT THE CAUSE OF THIS EFFECT --OR RATHER SAY, THE CAUSE OF THIS DEFECT.
PERPEND! I HAVE A DAUGHTER (HAVE WHILE SHE IS MINE), WHO IN HER DUTY AND OBEDIENCE, MARK, HATH GIVEN ME THIS.
"TO THE CELESTIAL, AND MY SOUL'S IDOL, THE MOST BEAUTIFIED OPHELIA--"
THAT'S AN ILL PHRASE, A VILE PHRASE--"BEAUTIFIED" IS A VILE PHRASE.
"IN HER EXCELLENT WHITE BOSOM..."
CAME THIS FROM HAMLET TO HER?
BUT HOW HATH SHE RECEIVED HIS LOVE?
WHAT DO YOU THINK OF ME?
AS OF A MAN FAITHFUL AND HONORABLE.
I WOULD FAIN PROVE SO. BUT WHAT MIGHT YOU THINK, HAD I SEEN THIS HOT LOVE ON THE WING, AND LOOKED UPON IT WITH IDLE SIGHT?

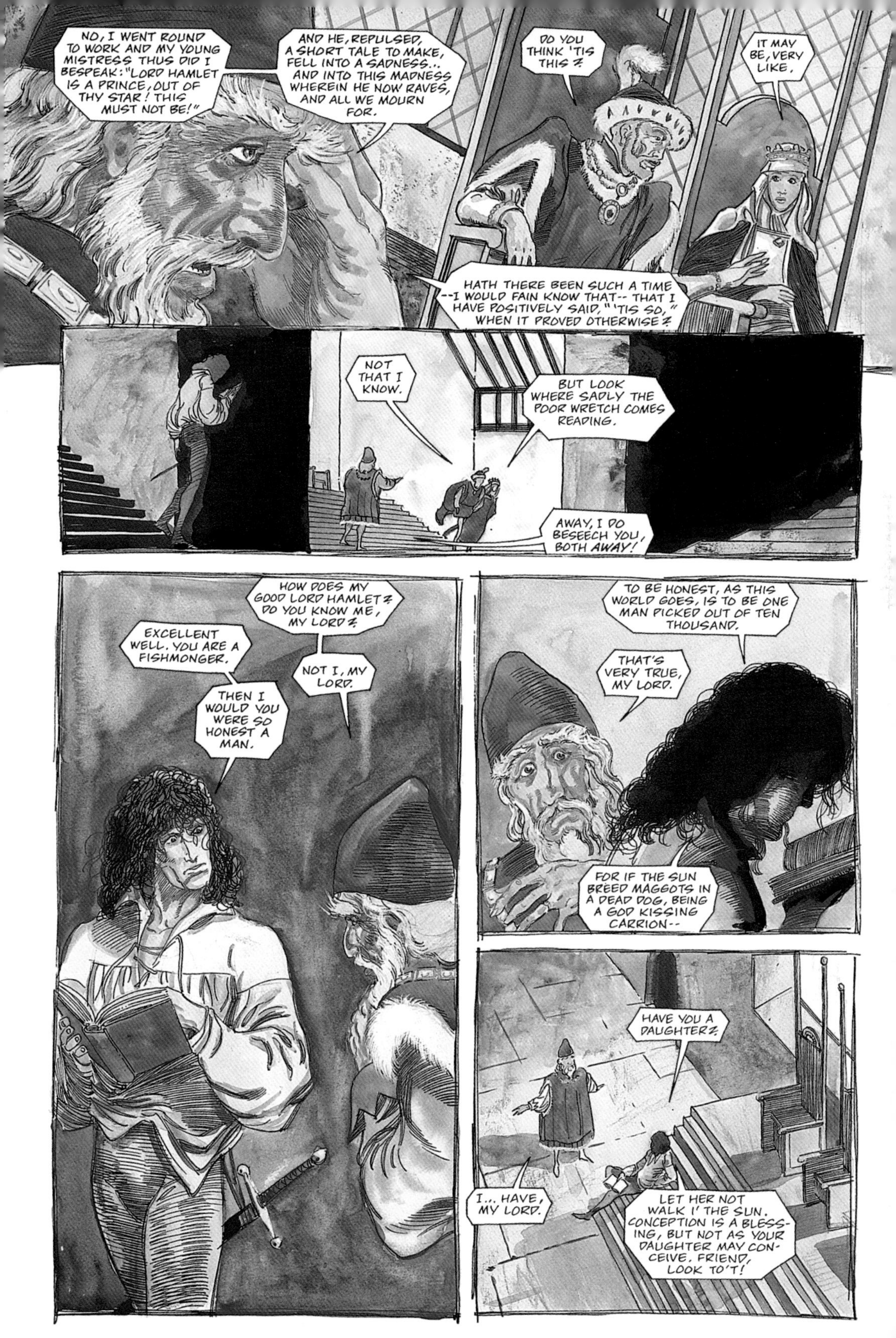
NO, I WENT ROUND TO WORK AND MY YOUNG MISTRESS THUS DID I BESPEAK: "LORD HAMLET IS A PRINCE, OUT OF THY STAR! THIS MUST NOT BE!"
AND HE, REPULSED, A SHORT TALE TO MAKE, FELL INTO A SADNESS... AND INTO THIS MADNESS WHEREIN HE NOW RAVES, AND ALL WE MOURN FOR.
DO YOU THINK 'TIS THIS?
IT MAY BE, VERY LIKE.
HATH THERE BEEN SUCH A TIME --I WOULD FAIN KNOW THAT-- THAT I HAVE POSITIVELY SAID, "'TIS SO," WHEN IT PROVED OTHERWISE?
NOT THAT I KNOW.
BUT LOOK WHERE SADLY THE POOR WRETCH COMES READING.
AWAY, I DO BESEECH YOU, BOTH AWAY!
HOW DOES MY GOOD LORD HAMLET? DO YOU KNOW ME, MY LORD?
EXCELLENT WELL. YOU ARE A FISHMONGER.
NOT I, MY LORD.
THEN I WOULD YOU WERE SO HONEST A MAN.
TO BE HONEST, AS THIS WORLD GOES, IS TO BE ONE MAN PICKED OUT OF TEN THOUSAND.
THAT'S VERY TRUE, MY LORD.
FOR IF THE SUN BREED MAGGOTS IN A DEAD DOG, BEING A GOD KISSING CARRION--
HAVE YOU A DAUGHTER?
I... HAVE, MY LORD.
LET HER NOT WALK I' THE SUN. CONCEPTION IS A BLESSING, BUT NOT AS YOUR DAUGHTER MAY CONCEIVE. FRIEND, LOOK TO'T!

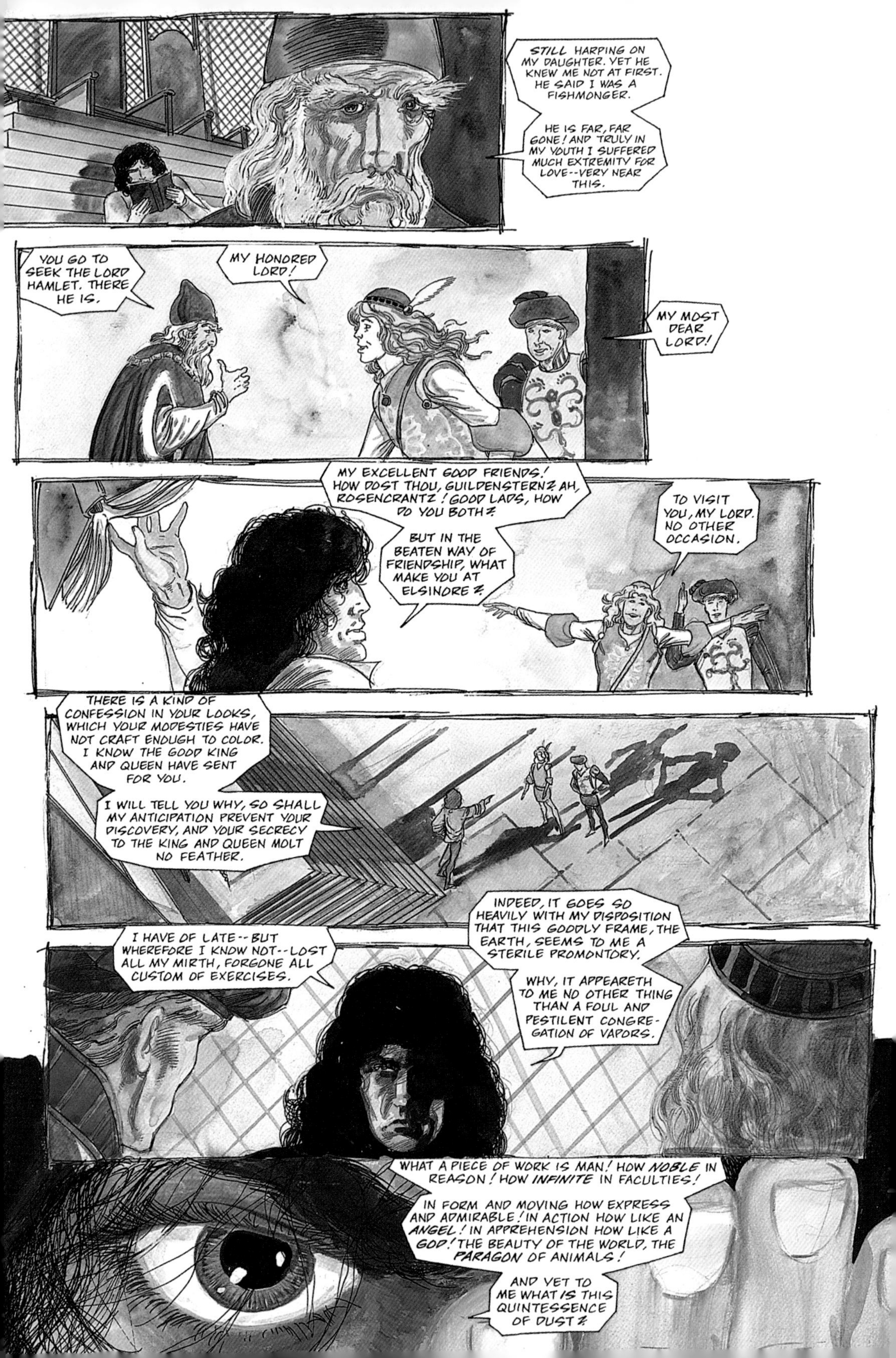
STILL HARPING ON MY DAUGHTER. YET HE KNEW ME NOT AT FIRST. HE SAID I WAS A FISHMONGER.
HE IS FAR, FAR GONE! AND TRULY IN MY YOUTH I SUFFERED MUCH EXTREMITY FOR LOVE--VERY NEAR THIS.
YOU GO TO SEEK THE LORD HAMLET. THERE HE IS.
MY HONORED LORD!
MY MOST DEAR LORD!
MY EXCELLENT GOOD FRIENDS! HOW DOST THOU, GUILDENSTERN? AH, ROSENCRANTZ! GOOD LADS, HOW DO YOU BOTH?
BUT IN THE BEATEN WAY OF FRIENDSHIP, WHAT MAKE YOU AT ELSINORE?
TO VISIT YOU, MY LORD. NO OTHER OCCASION.
THERE IS A KIND OF CONFESSION IN YOUR LOOKS, WHICH YOUR MODESTIES HAVE NOT CRAFT ENOUGH TO COLOR. I KNOW THE GOOD KING AND QUEEN HAVE SENT FOR YOU.
I WILL TELL YOU WHY, SO SHALL MY ANTICIPATION PREVENT YOUR DISCOVERY, AND YOUR SECRECY TO THE KING AND QUEEN MOLT NO FEATHER.
I HAVE OF LATE--BUT WHEREFORE I KNOW NOT--LOST ALL MY MIRTH, FORGONE ALL CUSTOM OF EXERCISES.
INDEED, IT GOES SO HEAVILY WITH MY DISPOSITION THAT THIS GOODLY FRAME, THE EARTH, SEEMS TO ME A STERILE PROMONTORY.
WHY, IT APPEARETH TO ME NO OTHER THING THAN A FOUL AND PESTILENT CONGREGATION OF VAPORS.
WHAT A PIECE OF WORK IS MAN! HOW NOBLE IN REASON! HOW INFINITE IN FACULTIES!
IN FORM AND MOVING HOW EXPRESS AND ADMIRABLE! IN ACTION HOW LIKE AN ANGEL! IN APPREHENSION HOW LIKE A GOD! THE BEAUTY OF THE WORLD, THE PARAGON OF ANIMALS!
AND YET TO ME WHAT IS THIS QUINTESSENCE OF DUST?

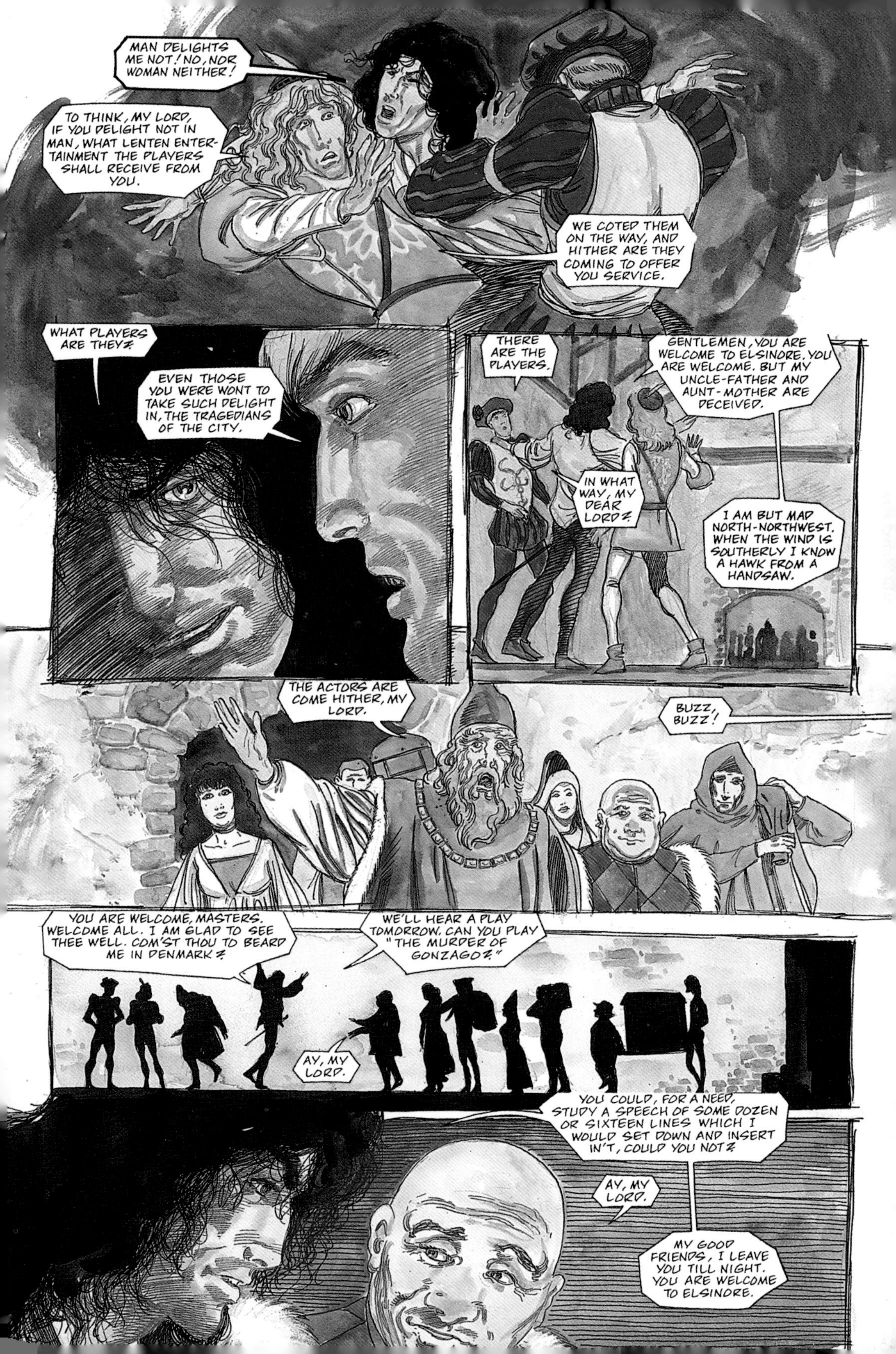
MAN DELIGHTS ME NOT! NO, NOR WOMAN NEITHER!
TO THINK, MY LORD, IF YOU DELIGHT NOT IN MAN, WHAT LENTEN ENTERTAINMENT THE PLAYERS SHALL RECEIVE FROM YOU.
WE COTED THEM ON THE WAY, AND HITHER ARE THEY COMING TO OFFER YOU SERVICE.
WHAT PLAYERS ARE THEY?
EVEN THOSE YOU WERE WONT TO TAKE SUCH DELIGHT IN, THE TRAGEDIANS OF THE CITY.
THERE ARE THE PLAYERS.
GENTLEMEN, YOU ARE WELCOME TO ELSINORE. YOU ARE WELCOME. BUT MY UNCLE-FATHER AND AUNT-MOTHER ARE DECEIVED.
IN WHAT WAY, MY DEAR LORD?
I AM BUT MAD NORTH-NORTHWEST. WHEN THE WIND IS SOUTHERLY I KNOW A HAWK FROM A HANDSAW.
THE ACTORS ARE COME HITHER, MY LORD.
BUZZ, BUZZ!
YOU ARE WELCOME, MASTERS. WELCOME ALL. I AM GLAD TO SEE THEE WELL. COM'ST THOU TO BEARD ME IN DENMARK?
WE'LL HEAR A PLAY TOMORROW. CAN YOU PLAY "THE MURDER OF GONZAGO?"
AY, MY LORD.
YOU COULD, FOR A NEED, STUDY A SPEECH OF SOME DOZEN OR SIXTEEN LINES WHICH I WOULD SET DOWN AND INSERT IN'T, COULD YOU NOT?
AY, MY LORD.
MY GOOD FRIENDS, I LEAVE YOU TILL NIGHT. YOU ARE WELCOME TO ELSINORE.

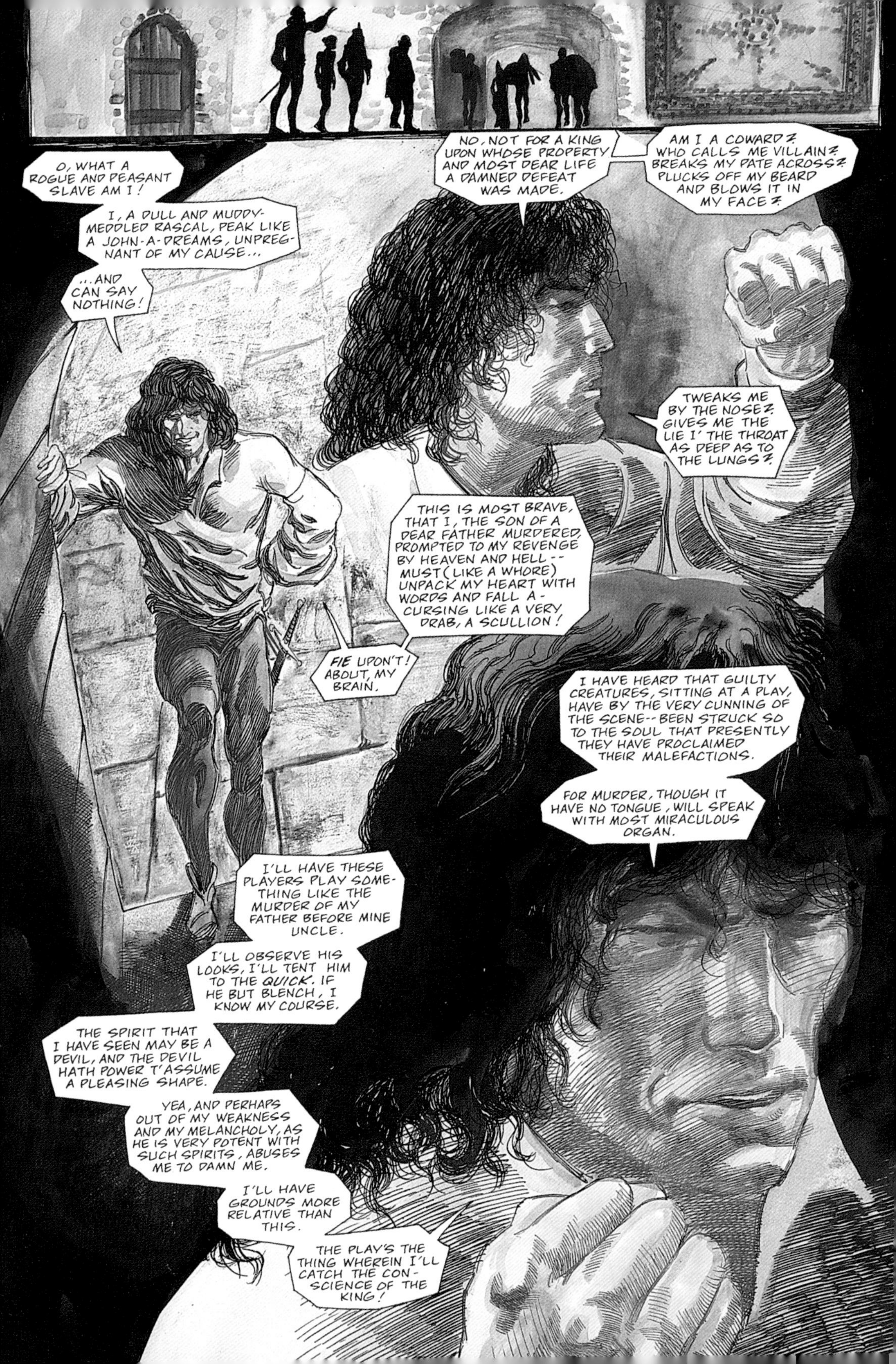
O, WHAT A ROGUE AND PEASANT SLAVE AM I!
I, A DULL AND MUDDY-MEDDLED RASCAL, PEAK LIKE A JOHN-A-DREAMS, UNPREGNANT OF MY CAUSE...
...AND CAN SAY NOTHING!
NO, NOT FOR A KING UPON WHOSE PROPERTY AND MOST DEAR LIFE A DAMNED DEFEAT WAS MADE.
AM I A COWARD? WHO CALLS ME VILLAIN? BREAKS MY PATE ACROSS? PLUCKS OFF MY BEARD AND BLOWS IT IN MY FACE?
TWEAKS ME BY THE NOSE? GIVES ME THE LIE I' THE THROAT AS DEEP AS TO THE LUNGS?
THIS IS MOST BRAVE, THAT I, THE SON OF A DEAR FATHER MURDERED, PROMPTED TO MY REVENGE BY HEAVEN AND HELL -- MUST (LIKE A WHORE) UNPACK MY HEART WITH WORDS AND FALL A-CURSING LIKE A VERY DRAB, A SCULLION!
FIE UPON'T! ABOUT, MY BRAIN.
I HAVE HEARD THAT GUILTY CREATURES, SITTING AT A PLAY, HAVE BY THE VERY CUNNING OF THE SCENE -- BEEN STRUCK SO TO THE SOUL THAT PRESENTLY THEY HAVE PROCLAIMED THEIR MALEFACTIONS.
FOR MURDER, THOUGH IT HAVE NO TONGUE, WILL SPEAK WITH MOST MIRACULOUS ORGAN.
I'LL HAVE THESE PLAYERS PLAY SOMETHING LIKE THE MURDER OF MY FATHER BEFORE MINE UNCLE.
I'LL OBSERVE HIS LOOKS, I'LL TENT HIM TO THE QUICK. IF HE BUT BLENCH, I KNOW MY COURSE.
THE SPIRIT THAT I HAVE SEEN MAY BE A DEVIL, AND THE DEVIL HATH POWER T'ASSUME A PLEASING SHAPE.
YEA, AND PERHAPS OUT OF MY WEAKNESS AND MY MELANCHOLY, AS HE IS VERY POTENT WITH SUCH SPIRITS, ABUSES ME TO DAMN ME.
I'LL HAVE GROUNDS MORE RELATIVE THAN THIS.
THE PLAY'S THE THING WHEREIN I'LL CATCH THE CONSCIENCE OF THE KING!

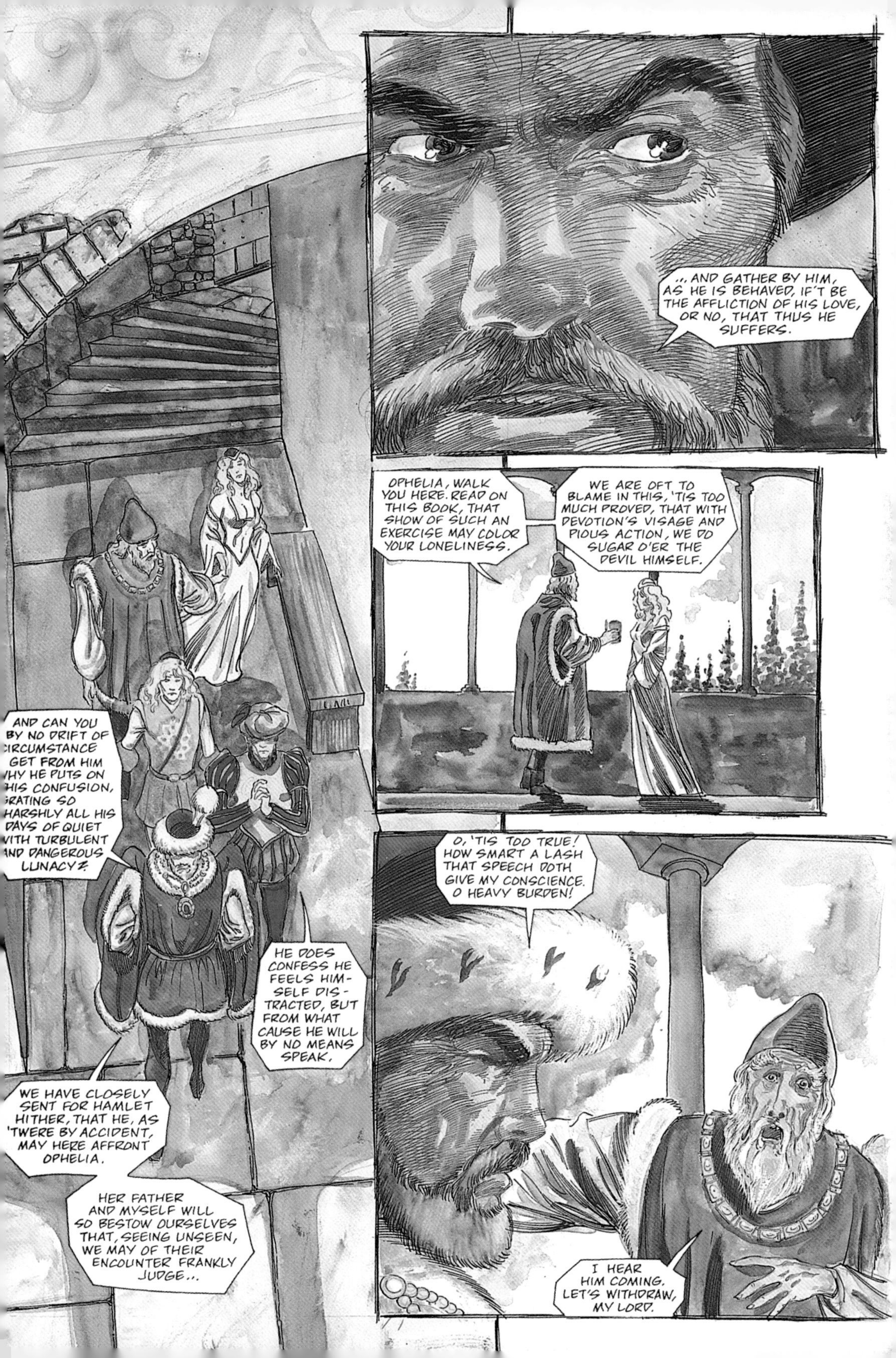

AND CAN YOU BY NO DRIFT OF CIRCUMSTANCE GET FROM HIM WHY HE PUTS ON THIS CONFUSION, GRATING SO HARSHLY ALL HIS DAYS OF QUIET WITH TURBULENT AND DANGEROUS LUNACY?
HE DOES CONFESS HE FEELS HIMSELF DISTRACTED, BUT FROM WHAT CAUSE HE WILL BY NO MEANS SPEAK.
WE HAVE CLOSELY SENT FOR HAMLET HITHER, THAT HE, AS 'TWERE BY ACCIDENT, MAY HERE AFFRONT OPHELIA.
HER FATHER AND MYSELF WILL SO BESTOW OURSELVES THAT, SEEING UNSEEN, WE MAY OF THEIR ENCOUNTER FRANKLY JUDGE...
...AND GATHER BY HIM, AS HE IS BEHAVED, IF'T BE THE AFFLICTION OF HIS LOVE, OR NO, THAT THUS HE SUFFERS.
OPHELIA, WALK YOU HERE. READ ON THIS BOOK, THAT SHOW OF SUCH AN EXERCISE MAY COLOR YOUR LONELINESS.
WE ARE OFT TO BLAME IN THIS, 'TIS TOO MUCH PROVED, THAT WITH DEVOTION'S VISAGE AND PIOUS ACTION, WE DO SUGAR O'ER THE DEVIL HIMSELF.
O, 'TIS TOO TRUE! HOW SMART A LASH THAT SPEECH DOTH GIVE MY CONSCIENCE. O HEAVY BURDEN!
I HEAR HIM COMING. LET'S WITHDRAW, MY LORD.

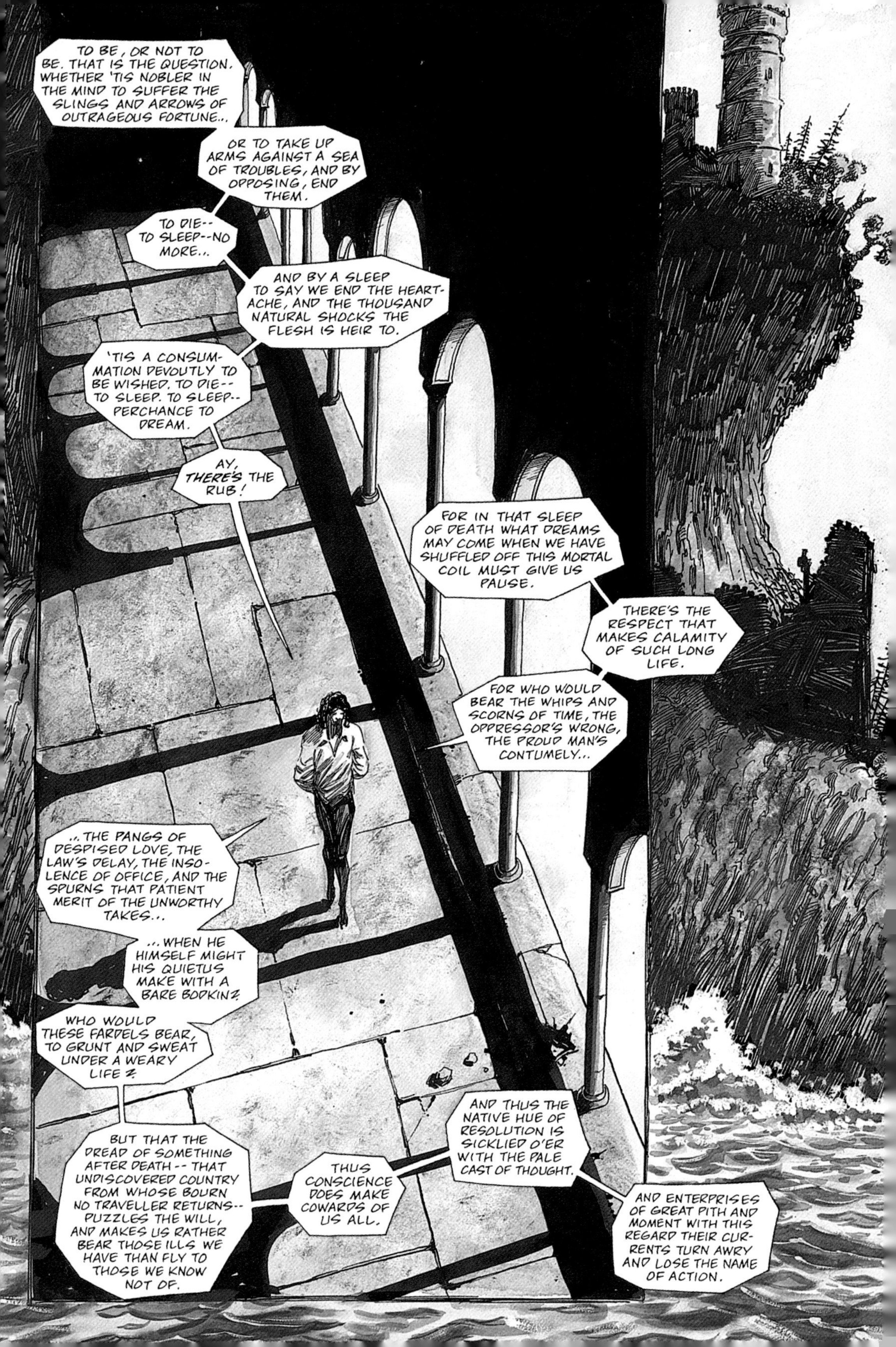

TO BE, OR NOT TO BE. THAT IS THE QUESTION. WHETHER 'TIS NOBLER IN THE MIND TO SUFFER THE SLINGS AND ARROWS OF OUTRAGEOUS FORTUNE...
OR TO TAKE UP ARMS AGAINST A SEA OF TROUBLES, AND BY OPPOSING, END THEM.
TO DIE-- TO SLEEP--NO MORE...
AND BY A SLEEP TO SAY WE END THE HEART-ACHE, AND THE THOUSAND NATURAL SHOCKS THE FLESH IS HEIR TO.
'TIS A CONSUMMATION DEVOUTLY TO BE WISHED. TO DIE-- TO SLEEP. TO SLEEP-- PERCHANCE TO DREAM.
AY, *THERE'S* THE RUB!
FOR IN THAT SLEEP OF DEATH WHAT DREAMS MAY COME WHEN WE HAVE SHUFFLED OFF THIS MORTAL COIL MUST GIVE US PAUSE.
THERE'S THE RESPECT THAT MAKES CALAMITY OF SUCH LONG LIFE.
FOR WHO WOULD BEAR THE WHIPS AND SCORNS OF TIME, THE OPPRESSOR'S WRONG, THE PROUD MAN'S CONTUMELY...
...THE PANGS OF DESPISED LOVE, THE LAW'S DELAY, THE INSOLENCE OF OFFICE, AND THE SPURNS THAT PATIENT MERIT OF THE UNWORTHY TAKES...
...WHEN HE HIMSELF MIGHT HIS QUIETUS MAKE WITH A BARE BODKIN?
WHO WOULD THESE FARDELS BEAR, TO GRUNT AND SWEAT UNDER A WEARY LIFE?
BUT THAT THE DREAD OF SOMETHING AFTER DEATH -- THAT UNDISCOVERED COUNTRY FROM WHOSE BOURN NO TRAVELLER RETURNS-- PUZZLES THE WILL, AND MAKES US RATHER BEAR THOSE ILLS WE HAVE THAN FLY TO THOSE WE KNOW NOT OF.
THUS CONSCIENCE DOES MAKE COWARDS OF US ALL.
AND THUS THE NATIVE HUE OF RESOLUTION IS SICKLIED O'ER WITH THE PALE CAST OF THOUGHT.
AND ENTERPRISES OF GREAT PITH AND MOMENT WITH THIS REGARD THEIR CURRENTS TURN AWRY AND LOSE THE NAME OF ACTION.

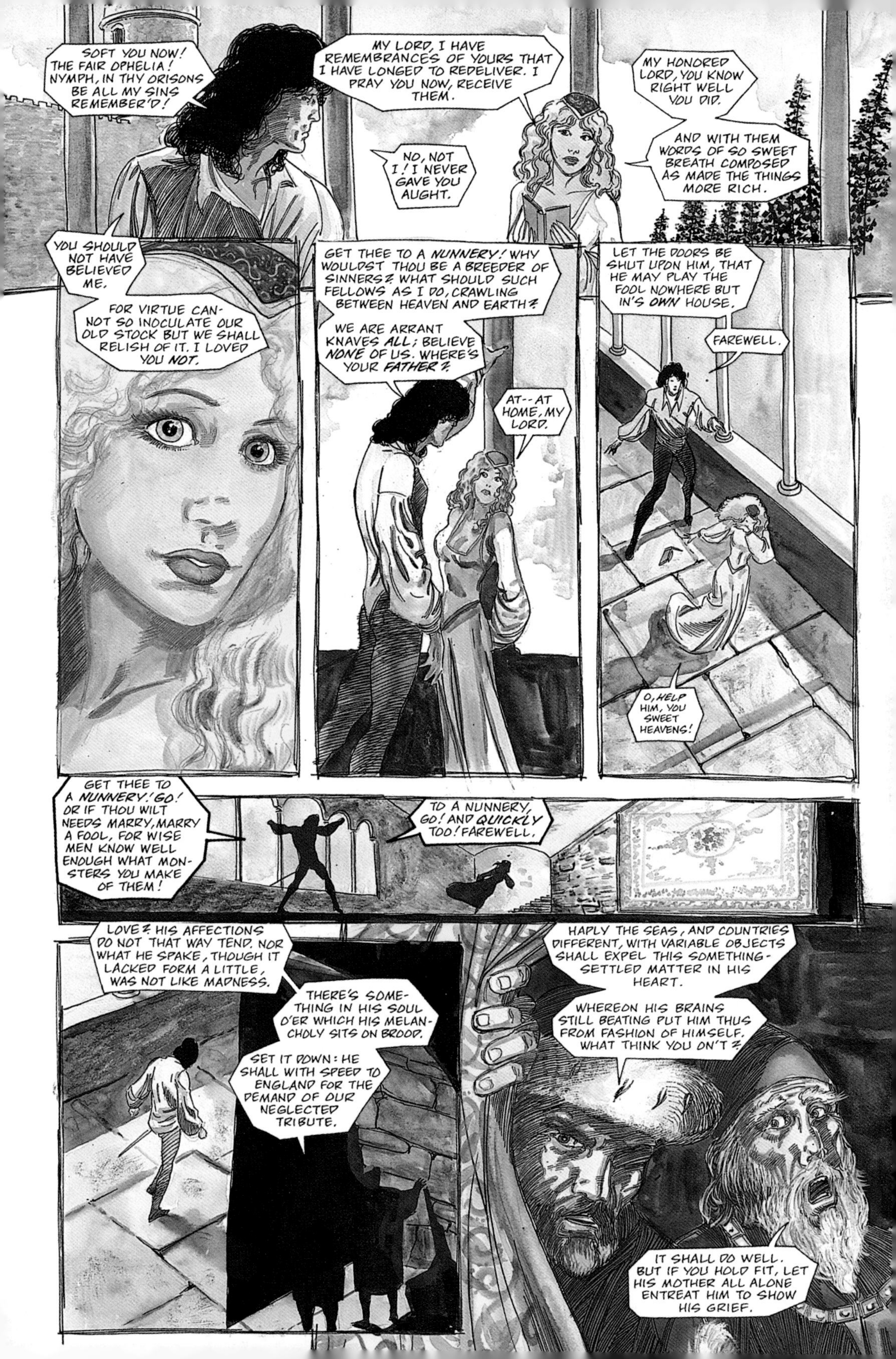

SOFT YOU NOW! THE FAIR OPHELIA! NYMPH, IN THY ORISONS BE ALL MY SINS REMEMBER'D!
MY LORD, I HAVE REMEMBRANCES OF YOURS THAT I HAVE LONGED TO REDELIVER. I PRAY YOU NOW, RECEIVE THEM.
NO, NOT I! I NEVER GAVE YOU AUGHT.
MY HONORED LORD, YOU KNOW RIGHT WELL YOU DID.
AND WITH THEM WORDS OF SO SWEET BREATH COMPOSED AS MADE THE THINGS MORE RICH.
YOU SHOULD NOT HAVE BELIEVED ME.
FOR VIRTUE CANNOT SO INOCULATE OUR OLD STOCK BUT WE SHALL RELISH OF IT. I LOVED YOU NOT.
GET THEE TO A NUNNERY! WHY WOULDST THOU BE A BREEDER OF SINNERS? WHAT SHOULD SUCH FELLOWS AS I DO, CRAWLING BETWEEN HEAVEN AND EARTH?
WE ARE ARRANT KNAVES ALL; BELIEVE NONE OF US. WHERE'S YOUR FATHER?
AT--AT HOME, MY LORD.
LET THE DOORS BE SHUT UPON HIM, THAT HE MAY PLAY THE FOOL NOWHERE BUT IN'S OWN HOUSE.
FAREWELL.
O, HELP HIM, YOU SWEET HEAVENS!
GET THEE TO A NUNNERY! GO! OR IF THOU WILT NEEDS MARRY, MARRY A FOOL, FOR WISE MEN KNOW WELL ENOUGH WHAT MONSTERS YOU MAKE OF THEM!
TO A NUNNERY, GO! AND QUICKLY TOO! FAREWELL.
LOVE? HIS AFFECTIONS DO NOT THAT WAY TEND. NOR WHAT HE SPAKE, THOUGH IT LACKED FORM A LITTLE, WAS NOT LIKE MADNESS.
THERE'S SOMETHING IN HIS SOUL O'ER WHICH HIS MELANCHOLY SITS ON BROOD.
SET IT DOWN: HE SHALL WITH SPEED TO ENGLAND FOR THE DEMAND OF OUR NEGLECTED TRIBUTE.
HAPLY THE SEAS, AND COUNTRIES DIFFERENT, WITH VARIABLE OBJECTS SHALL EXPEL THIS SOMETHING-SETTLED MATTER IN HIS HEART.
WHEREON HIS BRAINS STILL BEATING PUT HIM THUS FROM FASHION OF HIMSELF. WHAT THINK YOU ON'T?
IT SHALL DO WELL. BUT IF YOU HOLD FIT, LET HIS MOTHER ALL ALONE ENTREAT HIM TO SHOW HIS GRIEF.

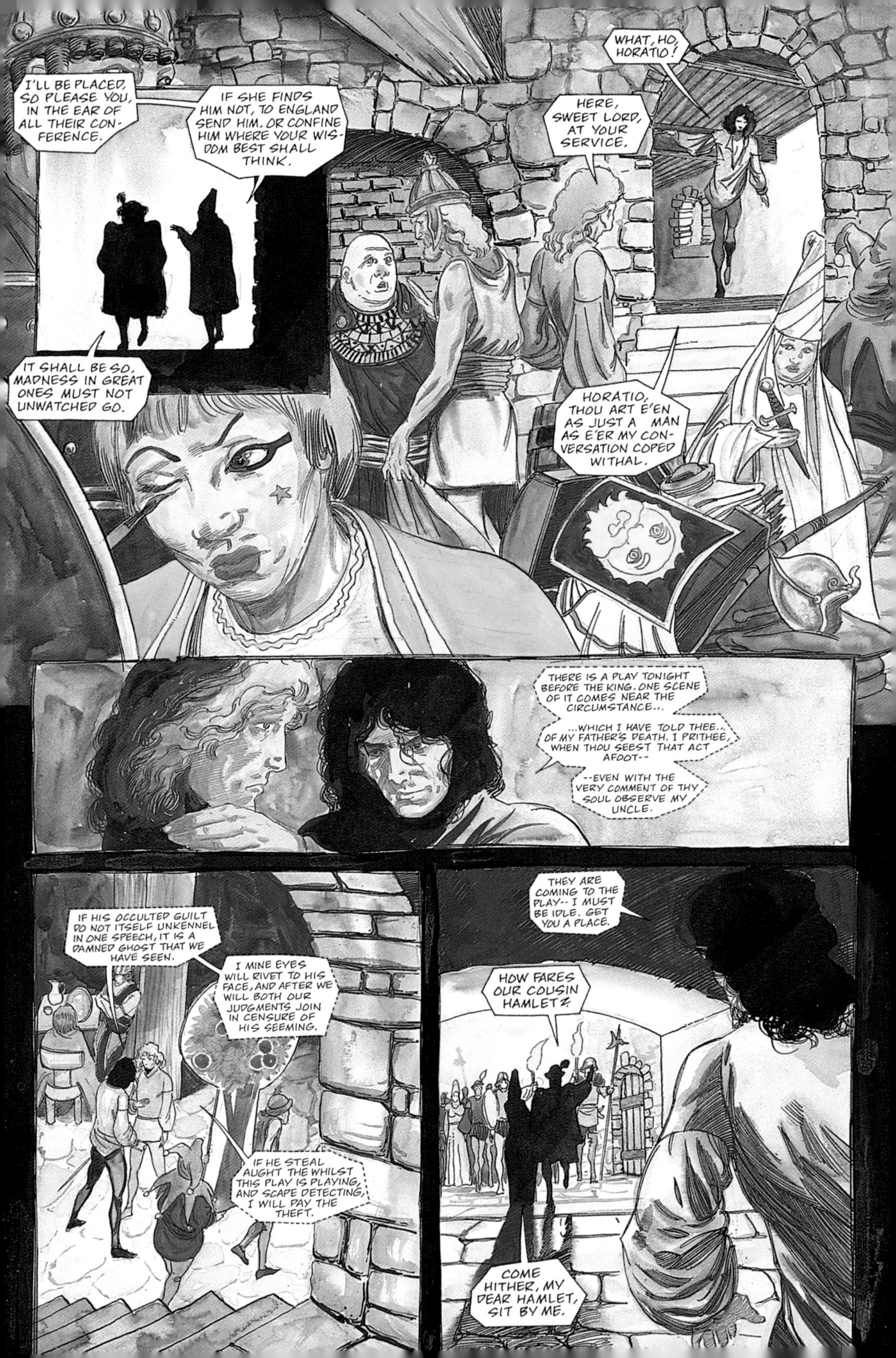
I'LL BE PLACED, SO PLEASE YOU, IN THE EAR OF ALL THEIR CONFERENCE.
IF SHE FINDS HIM NOT, TO ENGLAND SEND HIM. OR CONFINE HIM WHERE YOUR WISDOM BEST SHALL THINK.
IT SHALL BE SO. MADNESS IN GREAT ONES MUST NOT UNWATCHED GO.
WHAT, HO, HORATIO!
HERE, SWEET LORD, AT YOUR SERVICE.
HORATIO, THOU ART E'EN AS JUST A MAN AS E'ER MY CONVERSATION COPED WITHAL.
THERE IS A PLAY TONIGHT BEFORE THE KING. ONE SCENE OF IT COMES NEAR THE CIRCUMSTANCE...
...WHICH I HAVE TOLD THEE... OF MY FATHER'S DEATH. I PRITHEE, WHEN THOU SEEST THAT ACT AFOOT--
--EVEN WITH THE VERY COMMENT OF THY SOUL OBSERVE MY UNCLE.
IF HIS OCCULTED GUILT DO NOT ITSELF UNKENNEL IN ONE SPEECH, IT IS A DAMNED GHOST THAT WE HAVE SEEN.
I MINE EYES WILL RIVET TO HIS FACE, AND AFTER WE WILL BOTH OUR JUDGMENTS JOIN IN CENSURE OF HIS SEEMING.
IF HE STEAL AUGHT THE WHILST THIS PLAY IS PLAYING, AND SCAPE DETECTING, I WILL PAY THE THEFT.
THEY ARE COMING TO THE PLAY-- I MUST BE IDLE. GET YOU A PLACE.
HOW FARES OUR COUSIN HAMLET?
COME HITHER, MY DEAR HAMLET, SIT BY ME.

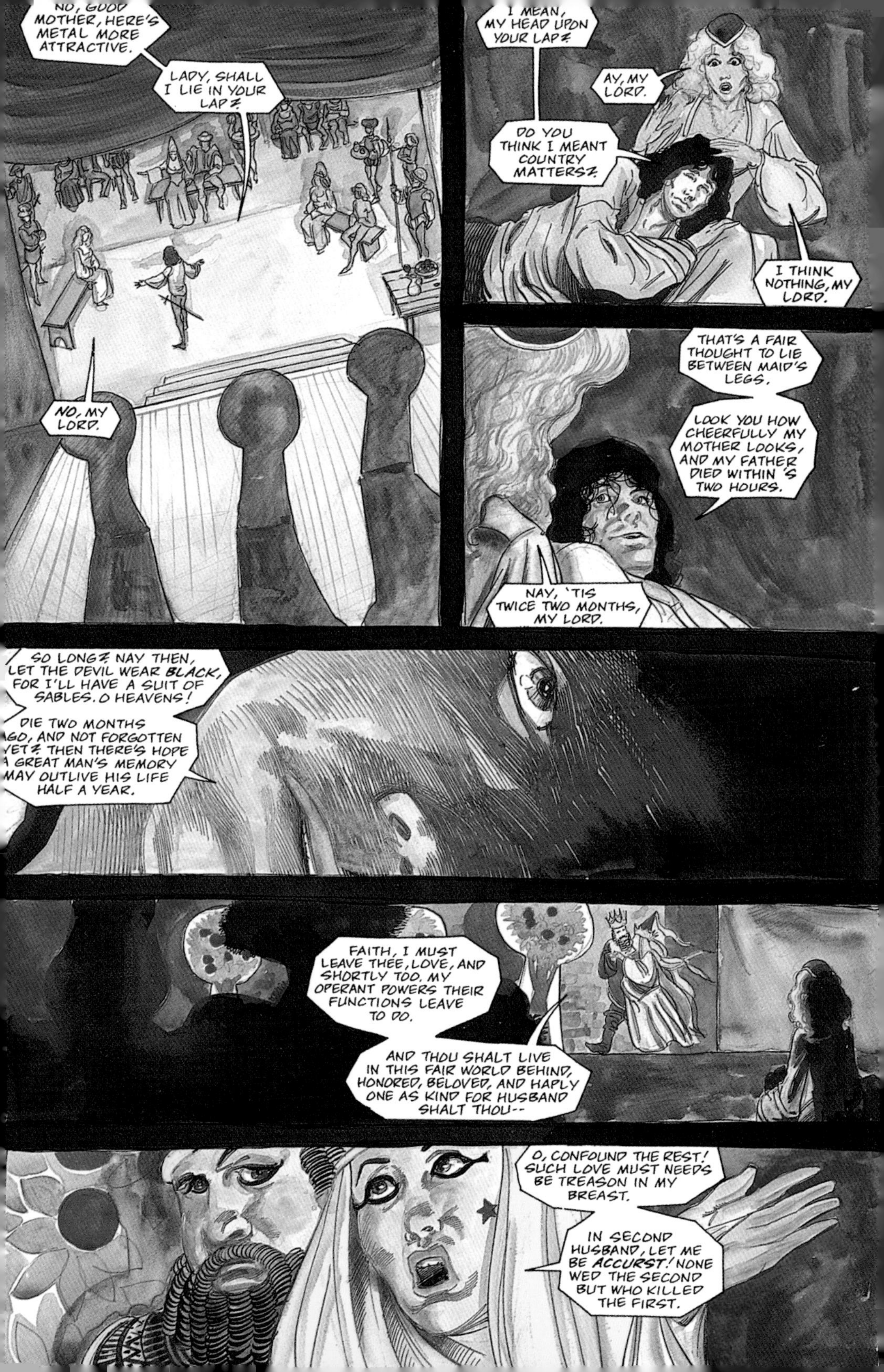
NO, GOOD MOTHER, HERE'S METAL MORE ATTRACTIVE.
LADY, SHALL I LIE IN YOUR LAP?
NO, MY LORD.
I MEAN, MY HEAD UPON YOUR LAP?
AY, MY LORD.
DO YOU THINK I MEANT COUNTRY MATTERS?
I THINK NOTHING, MY LORD.
THAT'S A FAIR THOUGHT TO LIE BETWEEN MAID'S LEGS.
LOOK YOU HOW CHEERFULLY MY MOTHER LOOKS, AND MY FATHER DIED WITHIN 'S TWO HOURS.
NAY, 'TIS TWICE TWO MONTHS, MY LORD.
SO LONG? NAY THEN, LET THE DEVIL WEAR BLACK, FOR I'LL HAVE A SUIT OF SABLES. O HEAVENS!
DIE TWO MONTHS AGO, AND NOT FORGOTTEN YET? THEN THERE'S HOPE A GREAT MAN'S MEMORY MAY OUTLIVE HIS LIFE HALF A YEAR.
FAITH, I MUST LEAVE THEE, LOVE, AND SHORTLY TOO. MY OPERANT POWERS THEIR FUNCTIONS LEAVE TO DO.
AND THOU SHALT LIVE IN THIS FAIR WORLD BEHIND, HONORED, BELOVED, AND HAPLY ONE AS KIND FOR HUSBAND SHALT THOU--
O, CONFOUND THE REST! SUCH LOVE MUST NEEDS BE TREASON IN MY BREAST.
IN SECOND HUSBAND, LET ME BE ACCURST! NONE WED THE SECOND BUT WHO KILLED THE FIRST.

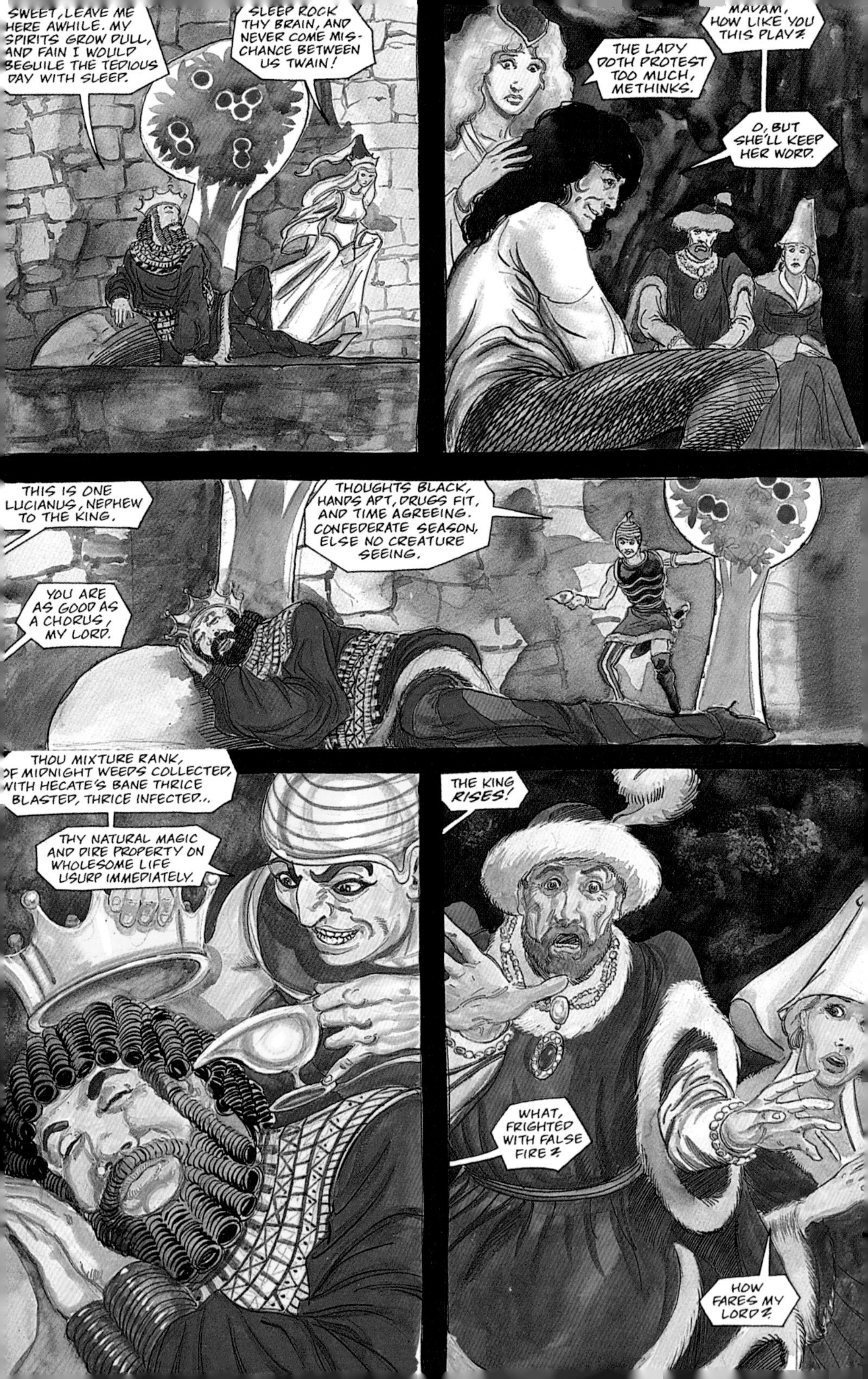
SWEET, LEAVE ME HERE AWHILE. MY SPIRITS GROW DULL, AND FAIN I WOULD BEGUILE THE TEDIOUS DAY WITH SLEEP.
SLEEP ROCK THY BRAIN, AND NEVER COME MISCHANCE BETWEEN US TWAIN!
MADAM, HOW LIKE YOU THIS PLAY?
THE LADY DOTH PROTEST TOO MUCH, METHINKS.
O, BUT SHE'LL KEEP HER WORD.
THIS IS ONE LUCIANUS, NEPHEW TO THE KING.
THOUGHTS BLACK, HANDS APT, DRUGS FIT, AND TIME AGREEING. CONFEDERATE SEASON, ELSE NO CREATURE SEEING.
YOU ARE AS GOOD AS A CHORUS, MY LORD.
THOU MIXTURE RANK, OF MIDNIGHT WEEDS COLLECTED, WITH HECATE'S BANE THRICE BLASTED, THRICE INFECTED...
THY NATURAL MAGIC AND DIRE PROPERTY ON WHOLESOME LIFE USURP IMMEDIATELY.
THE KING RISES!
WHAT, FRIGHTED WITH FALSE FIRE?
HOW FARES MY LORD?

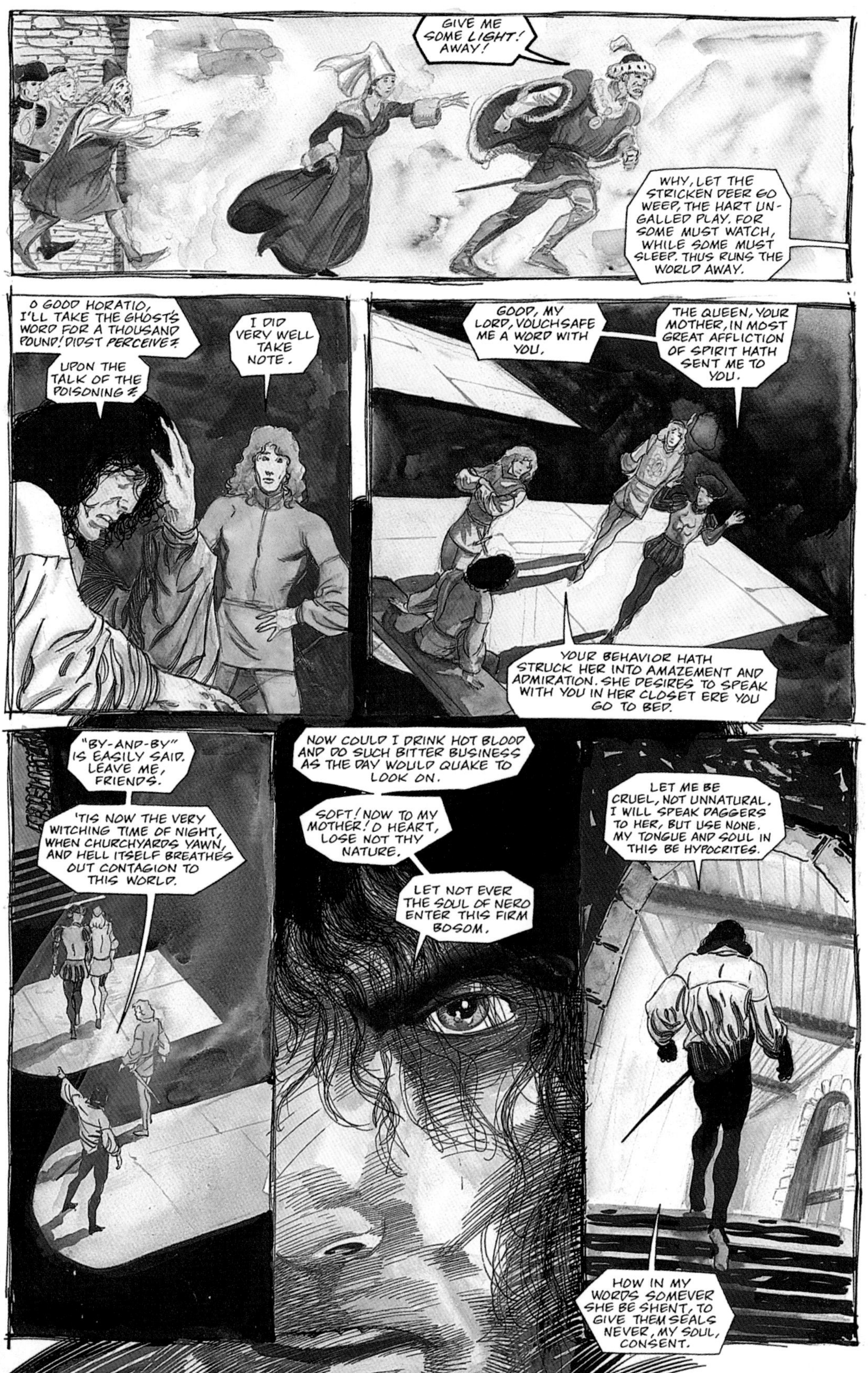
GIVE ME SOME LIGHT! AWAY!
WHY, LET THE STRICKEN DEER GO WEEP, THE HART UN-GALLED PLAY. FOR SOME MUST WATCH, WHILE SOME MUST SLEEP. THUS RUNS THE WORLD AWAY.
O GOOD HORATIO, I'LL TAKE THE GHOST'S WORD FOR A THOUSAND POUND! DIDST PERCEIVE?
I DID VERY WELL TAKE NOTE.
UPON THE TALK OF THE POISONING?
GOOD, MY LORD, VOUCHSAFE ME A WORD WITH YOU.
THE QUEEN, YOUR MOTHER, IN MOST GREAT AFFLICTION OF SPIRIT HATH SENT ME TO YOU.
YOUR BEHAVIOR HATH STRUCK HER INTO AMAZEMENT AND ADMIRATION. SHE DESIRES TO SPEAK WITH YOU IN HER CLOSET ERE YOU GO TO BED.
"BY-AND-BY" IS EASILY SAID. LEAVE ME, FRIENDS.
'TIS NOW THE VERY WITCHING TIME OF NIGHT, WHEN CHURCHYARDS YAWN, AND HELL ITSELF BREATHES OUT CONTAGION TO THIS WORLD.
NOW COULD I DRINK HOT BLOOD AND DO SUCH BITTER BUSINESS AS THE DAY WOULD QUAKE TO LOOK ON.
SOFT! NOW TO MY MOTHER! O HEART, LOSE NOT THY NATURE.
LET NOT EVER THE SOUL OF NERO ENTER THIS FIRM BOSOM.
LET ME BE CRUEL, NOT UNNATURAL. I WILL SPEAK DAGGERS TO HER, BUT USE NONE. MY TONGUE AND SOUL IN THIS BE HYPOCRITES.
HOW IN MY WORDS SOMEVER SHE BE SHENT, TO GIVE THEM SEALS NEVER, MY SOUL, CONSENT.

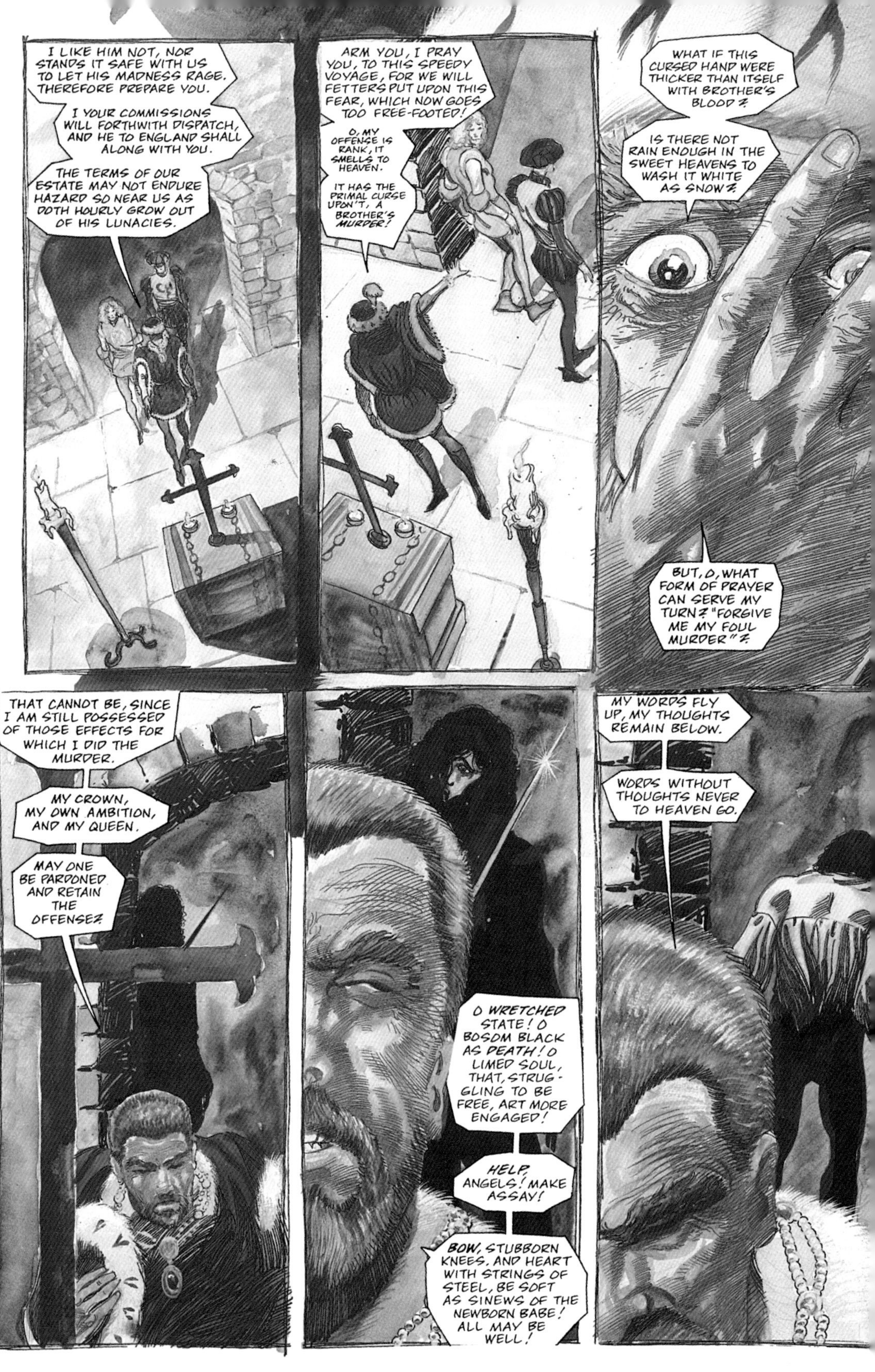
I LIKE HIM NOT, NOR STANDS IT SAFE WITH US TO LET HIS MADNESS RAGE. THEREFORE PREPARE YOU.
I YOUR COMMISSIONS WILL FORTHWITH DISPATCH, AND HE TO ENGLAND SHALL ALONG WITH YOU.
THE TERMS OF OUR ESTATE MAY NOT ENDURE HAZARD SO NEAR US AS DOTH HOURLY GROW OUT OF HIS LUNACIES.
ARM YOU, I PRAY YOU, TO THIS SPEEDY VOYAGE, FOR WE WILL FETTERS PUT UPON THIS FEAR, WHICH NOW GOES TOO FREE-FOOTED!
O, MY OFFENSE IS RANK, IT SMELLS TO HEAVEN.
IT HAS THE PRIMAL CURSE UPON'T, A BROTHER'S MURDER!
WHAT IF THIS CURSED HAND WERE THICKER THAN ITSELF WITH BROTHER'S BLOOD?
IS THERE NOT RAIN ENOUGH IN THE SWEET HEAVENS TO WASH IT WHITE AS SNOW?
BUT, O, WHAT FORM OF PRAYER CAN SERVE MY TURN? "FORGIVE ME MY FOUL MURDER"?
THAT CANNOT BE, SINCE I AM STILL POSSESSED OF THOSE EFFECTS FOR WHICH I DID THE MURDER.
MY CROWN, MY OWN AMBITION, AND MY QUEEN.
MAY ONE BE PARDONED AND RETAIN THE OFFENSE?
O WRETCHED STATE! O BOSOM BLACK AS DEATH! O LIMED SOUL, THAT, STRUG-GLING TO BE FREE, ART MORE ENGAGED!
HELP, ANGELS! MAKE ASSAY!
BOW, STUBBORN KNEES. AND HEART WITH STRINGS OF STEEL, BE SOFT AS SINEWS OF THE NEWBORN BABE! ALL MAY BE WELL!
MY WORDS FLY UP, MY THOUGHTS REMAIN BELOW.
WORDS WITHOUT THOUGHTS NEVER TO HEAVEN GO.

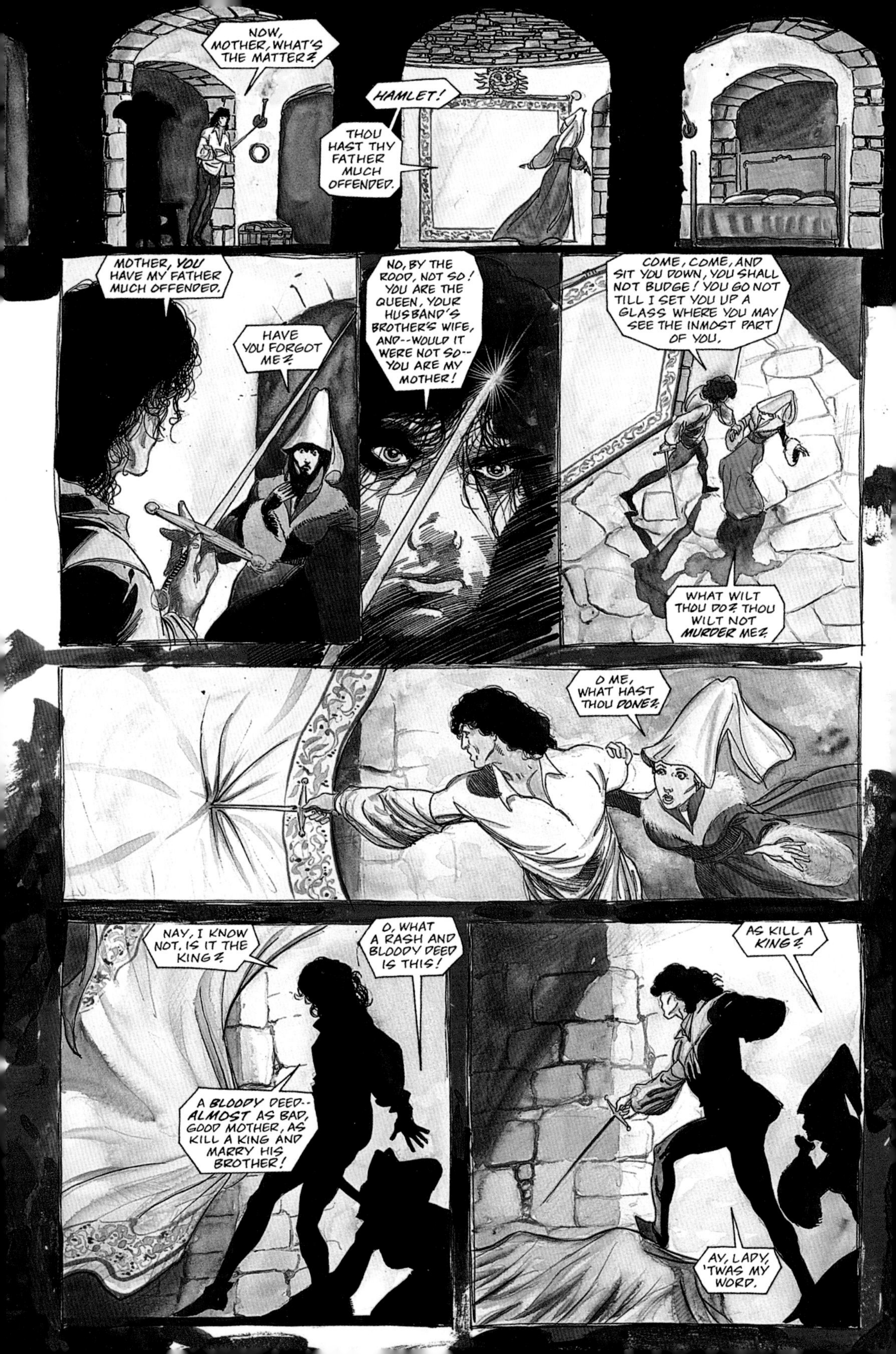
NOW, MOTHER, WHAT'S THE MATTER?
HAMLET!
THOU HAST THY FATHER MUCH OFFENDED.
MOTHER, YOU HAVE MY FATHER MUCH OFFENDED.
HAVE YOU FORGOT ME?
NO, BY THE ROOD, NOT SO! YOU ARE THE QUEEN, YOUR HUSBAND'S BROTHER'S WIFE, AND--WOULD IT WERE NOT SO--YOU ARE MY MOTHER!
COME, COME, AND SIT YOU DOWN, YOU SHALL NOT BUDGE! YOU GO NOT TILL I SET YOU UP A GLASS WHERE YOU MAY SEE THE INMOST PART OF YOU.
WHAT WILT THOU DO? THOU WILT NOT MURDER ME?
O ME, WHAT HAST THOU DONE?
NAY, I KNOW NOT. IS IT THE KING?
O, WHAT A RASH AND BLOODY DEED IS THIS!
A BLOODY DEED--ALMOST AS BAD, GOOD MOTHER, AS KILL A KING AND MARRY HIS BROTHER!
AS KILL A KING?
AY, LADY, 'TWAS MY WORD.

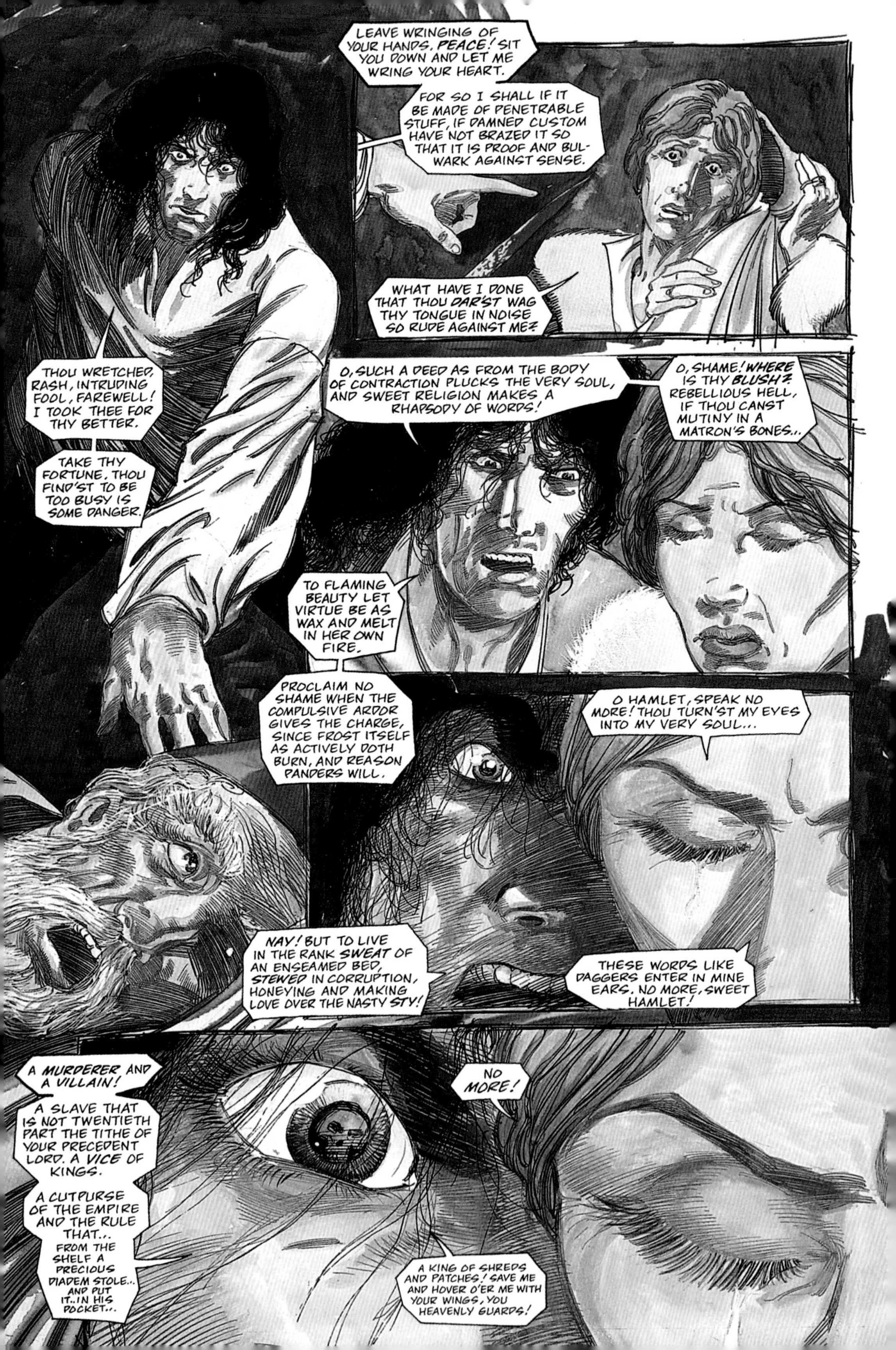

LEAVE WRINGING OF YOUR HANDS. PEACE! SIT YOU DOWN AND LET ME WRING YOUR HEART.
FOR SO I SHALL IF IT BE MADE OF PENETRABLE STUFF, IF DAMNED CUSTOM HAVE NOT BRAZED IT SO THAT IT IS PROOF AND BULWARK AGAINST SENSE.
WHAT HAVE I DONE THAT THOU DAR'ST WAG THY TONGUE IN NOISE SO RUDE AGAINST ME?
THOU WRETCHED, RASH, INTRUDING FOOL, FAREWELL! I TOOK THEE FOR THY BETTER.
TAKE THY FORTUNE. THOU FIND'ST TO BE TOO BUSY IS SOME DANGER.
O, SUCH A DEED AS FROM THE BODY OF CONTRACTION PLUCKS THE VERY SOUL, AND SWEET RELIGION MAKES A RHAPSODY OF WORDS!
O, SHAME! WHERE IS THY BLUSH? REBELLIOUS HELL, IF THOU CANST MUTINY IN A MATRON'S BONES...
TO FLAMING BEAUTY LET VIRTUE BE AS WAX AND MELT IN HER OWN FIRE.
PROCLAIM NO SHAME WHEN THE COMPULSIVE ARDOR GIVES THE CHARGE, SINCE FROST ITSELF AS ACTIVELY DOTH BURN, AND REASON PANDERS WILL.
O HAMLET, SPEAK NO MORE! THOU TURN'ST MY EYES INTO MY VERY SOUL...
NAY! BUT TO LIVE IN THE RANK SWEAT OF AN ENSEAMED BED, STEWED IN CORRUPTION, HONEYING AND MAKING LOVE OVER THE NASTY STY!
THESE WORDS LIKE DAGGERS ENTER IN MINE EARS. NO MORE, SWEET HAMLET!
A MURDERER AND A VILLAIN!
A SLAVE THAT IS NOT TWENTIETH PART THE TITHE OF YOUR PRECEDENT LORD. A VICE OF KINGS.
A CUTPURSE OF THE EMPIRE AND THE RULE THAT... FROM THE SHELF A PRECIOUS DIADEM STOLE... AND PUT IT... IN HIS POCKET...
NO MORE!
A KING OF SHREDS AND PATCHES! SAVE ME AND HOVER O'ER ME WITH YOUR WINGS, YOU HEAVENLY GUARDS!

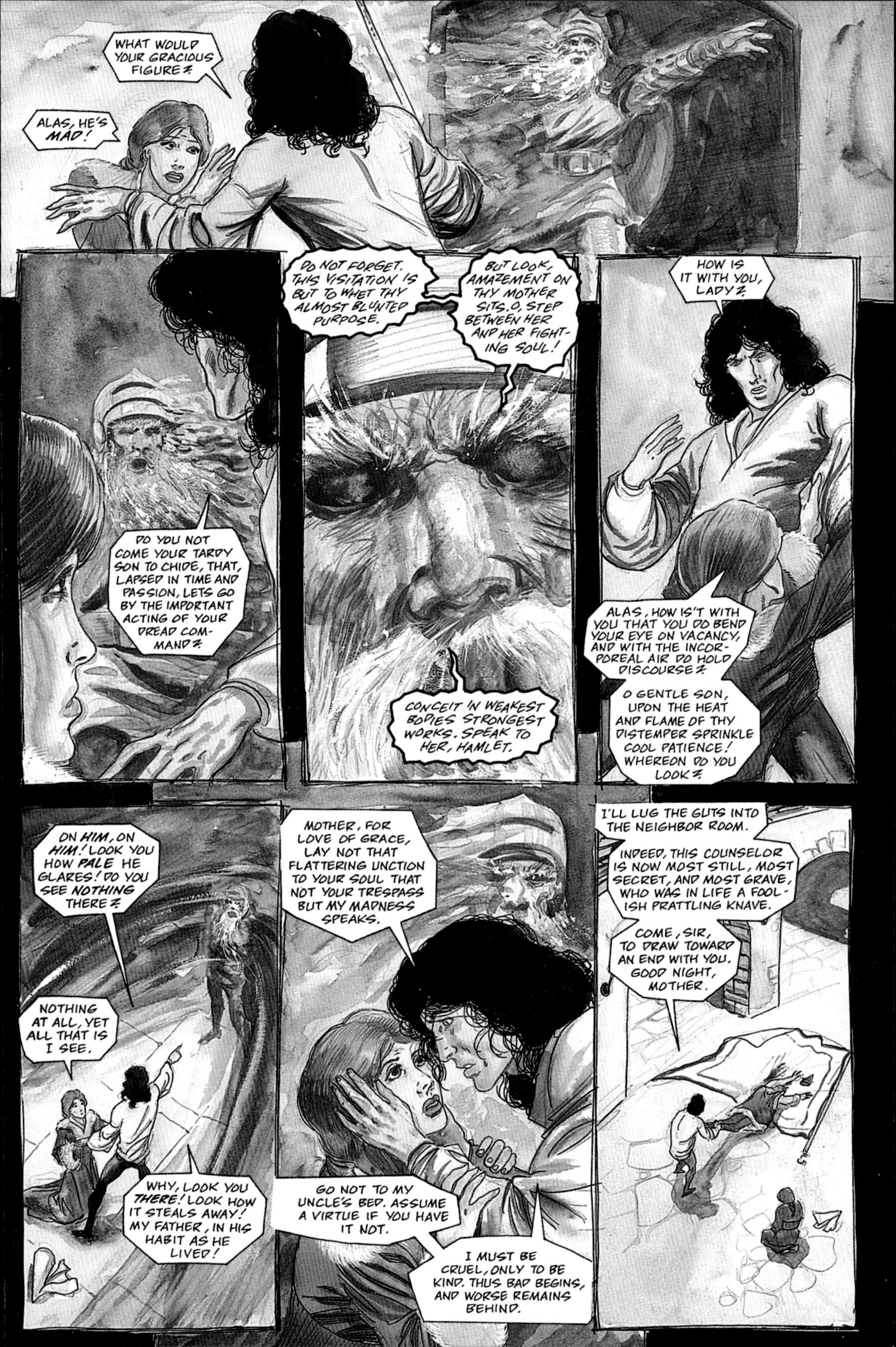
WHAT WOULD YOUR GRACIOUS FIGURE?
ALAS, HE'S *MAD*!
DO YOU NOT COME YOUR TARDY SON TO CHIDE, THAT, LAPSED IN TIME AND PASSION, LETS GO BY THE IMPORTANT ACTING OF YOUR DREAD COM-MAND?
DO NOT FORGET. THIS VISITATION IS BUT TO WHET THY ALMOST BLUNTED PURPOSE.
BUT LOOK, AMAZEMENT ON THY MOTHER SITS. O, STEP BETWEEN HER AND HER FIGHTING SOUL!
CONCEIT IN WEAKEST BODIES STRONGEST WORKS. SPEAK TO HER, HAMLET.
HOW IS IT WITH YOU, LADY?
ALAS, HOW IS'T WITH YOU THAT YOU DO BEND YOUR EYE ON VACANCY, AND WITH THE INCOR-POREAL AIR DO HOLD DISCOURSE?
O GENTLE SON, UPON THE HEAT AND FLAME OF THY DISTEMPER SPRINKLE COOL PATIENCE! WHEREON DO YOU LOOK?
ON *HIM*, ON *HIM*! LOOK YOU HOW *PALE* HE GLARES! DO YOU SEE *NOTHING* THERE?
NOTHING AT ALL, YET ALL THAT IS I SEE.
WHY, LOOK YOU *THERE*! LOOK HOW IT STEALS AWAY! MY FATHER, IN HIS HABIT AS HE LIVED!
MOTHER, FOR LOVE OF GRACE, LAY NOT THAT FLATTERING UNCTION TO YOUR SOUL THAT NOT YOUR TRESPASS BUT MY MADNESS SPEAKS.
GO NOT TO MY UNCLE'S BED. ASSUME A VIRTUE IF YOU HAVE IT NOT.
I MUST BE CRUEL, ONLY TO BE KIND. THUS BAD BEGINS, AND WORSE REMAINS BEHIND.
I'LL LUG THE GUTS INTO THE NEIGHBOR ROOM.
INDEED, THIS COUNSELOR IS NOW MOST STILL, MOST SECRET, AND MOST GRAVE, WHO WAS IN LIFE A FOOL-ISH PRATTLING KNAVE.
COME, SIR, TO DRAW TOWARD AN END WITH YOU. GOOD NIGHT, MOTHER.

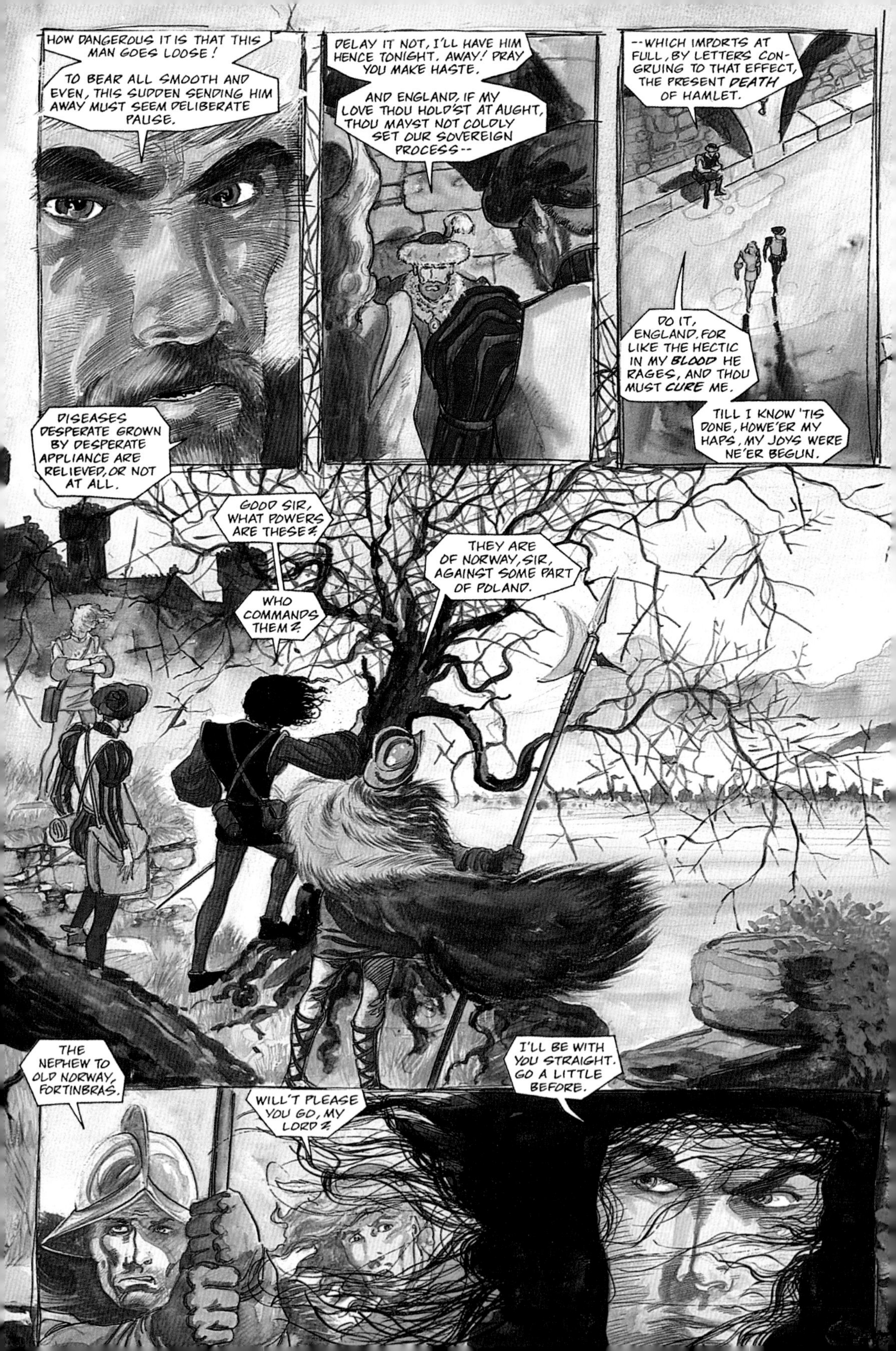
HOW DANGEROUS IT IS THAT THIS MAN GOES LOOSE!
TO BEAR ALL SMOOTH AND EVEN, THIS SUDDEN SENDING HIM AWAY MUST SEEM DELIBERATE PAUSE.
DISEASES DESPERATE GROWN BY DESPERATE APPLIANCE ARE RELIEVED, OR NOT AT ALL.
DELAY IT NOT, I'LL HAVE HIM HENCE TONIGHT. AWAY! PRAY YOU MAKE HASTE.
AND ENGLAND, IF MY LOVE THOU HOLD'ST AT AUGHT, THOU MAYST NOT COLDLY SET OUR SOVEREIGN PROCESS--
--WHICH IMPORTS AT FULL, BY LETTERS CONGRUING TO THAT EFFECT, THE PRESENT DEATH OF HAMLET.
DO IT, ENGLAND, FOR LIKE THE HECTIC IN MY BLOOD HE RAGES, AND THOU MUST CURE ME.
TILL I KNOW 'TIS DONE, HOWE'ER MY HAPS, MY JOYS WERE NE'ER BEGUN.
GOOD SIR, WHAT POWERS ARE THESE?
WHO COMMANDS THEM?
THEY ARE OF NORWAY, SIR, AGAINST SOME PART OF POLAND.
THE NEPHEW TO OLD NORWAY, FORTINBRAS.
WILL'T PLEASE YOU GO, MY LORD?
I'LL BE WITH YOU STRAIGHT. GO A LITTLE BEFORE.

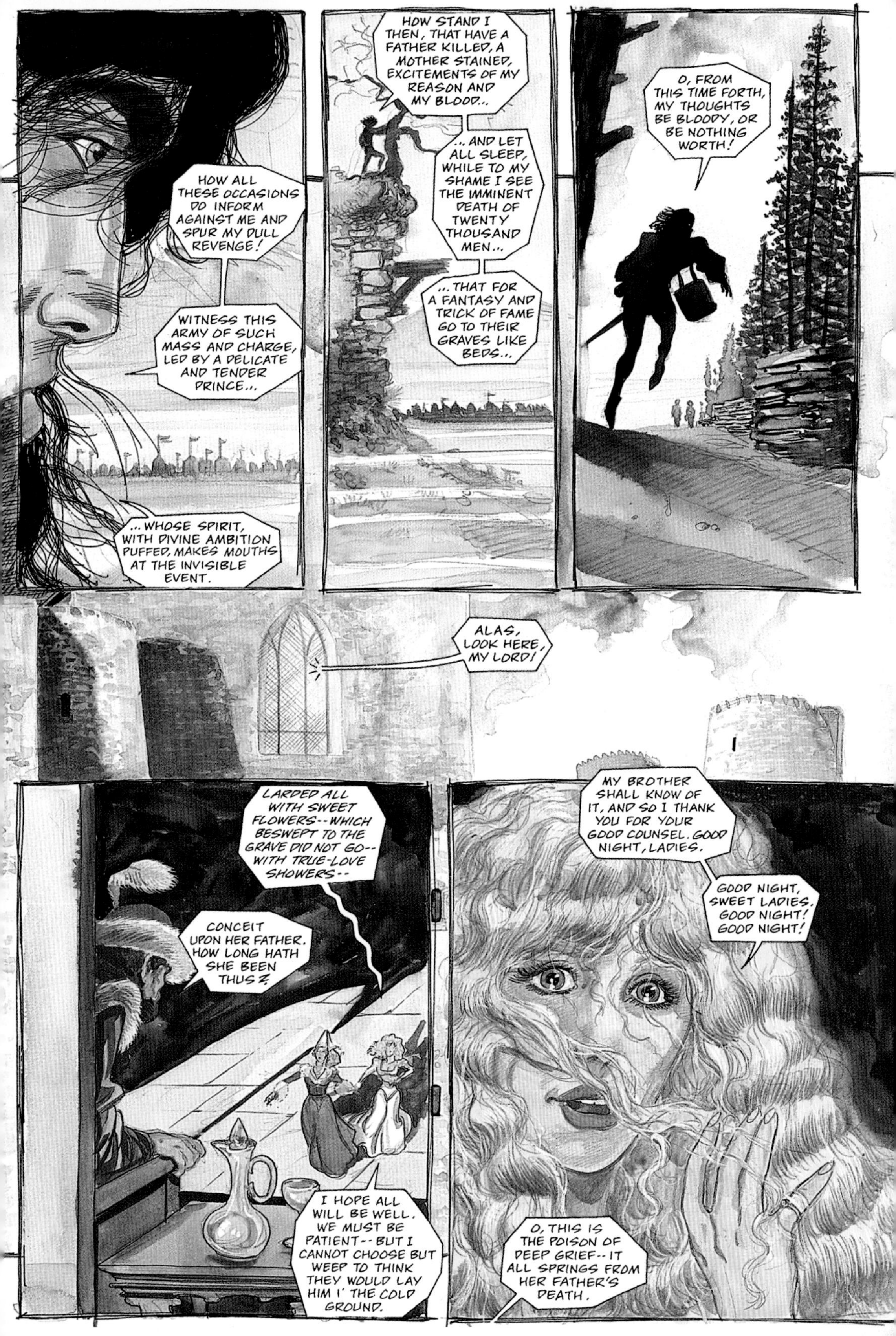

HOW ALL THESE OCCASIONS DO INFORM AGAINST ME AND SPUR MY DULL REVENGE!
WITNESS THIS ARMY OF SUCH MASS AND CHARGE, LED BY A DELICATE AND TENDER PRINCE...
...WHOSE SPIRIT, WITH DIVINE AMBITION PUFFED, MAKES MOUTHS AT THE INVISIBLE EVENT.
HOW STAND I THEN, THAT HAVE A FATHER KILLED, A MOTHER STAINED, EXCITEMENTS OF MY REASON AND MY BLOOD...
...AND LET ALL SLEEP, WHILE TO MY SHAME I SEE THE IMMINENT DEATH OF TWENTY THOUSAND MEN...
...THAT FOR A FANTASY AND TRICK OF FAME GO TO THEIR GRAVES LIKE BEDS...
O, FROM THIS TIME FORTH, MY THOUGHTS BE BLOODY, OR BE NOTHING WORTH!
ALAS, LOOK HERE, MY LORD!
LARDED ALL WITH SWEET FLOWERS--WHICH BESWEPT TO THE GRAVE DID NOT GO--WITH TRUE-LOVE SHOWERS--
CONCEIT UPON HER FATHER. HOW LONG HATH SHE BEEN THUS?
I HOPE ALL WILL BE WELL. WE MUST BE PATIENT--BUT I CANNOT CHOOSE BUT WEEP TO THINK THEY WOULD LAY HIM I' THE COLD GROUND.
MY BROTHER SHALL KNOW OF IT, AND SO I THANK YOU FOR YOUR GOOD COUNSEL. GOOD NIGHT, LADIES.
GOOD NIGHT, SWEET LADIES. GOOD NIGHT! GOOD NIGHT!
O, THIS IS THE POISON OF DEEP GRIEF--IT ALL SPRINGS FROM HER FATHER'S DEATH.

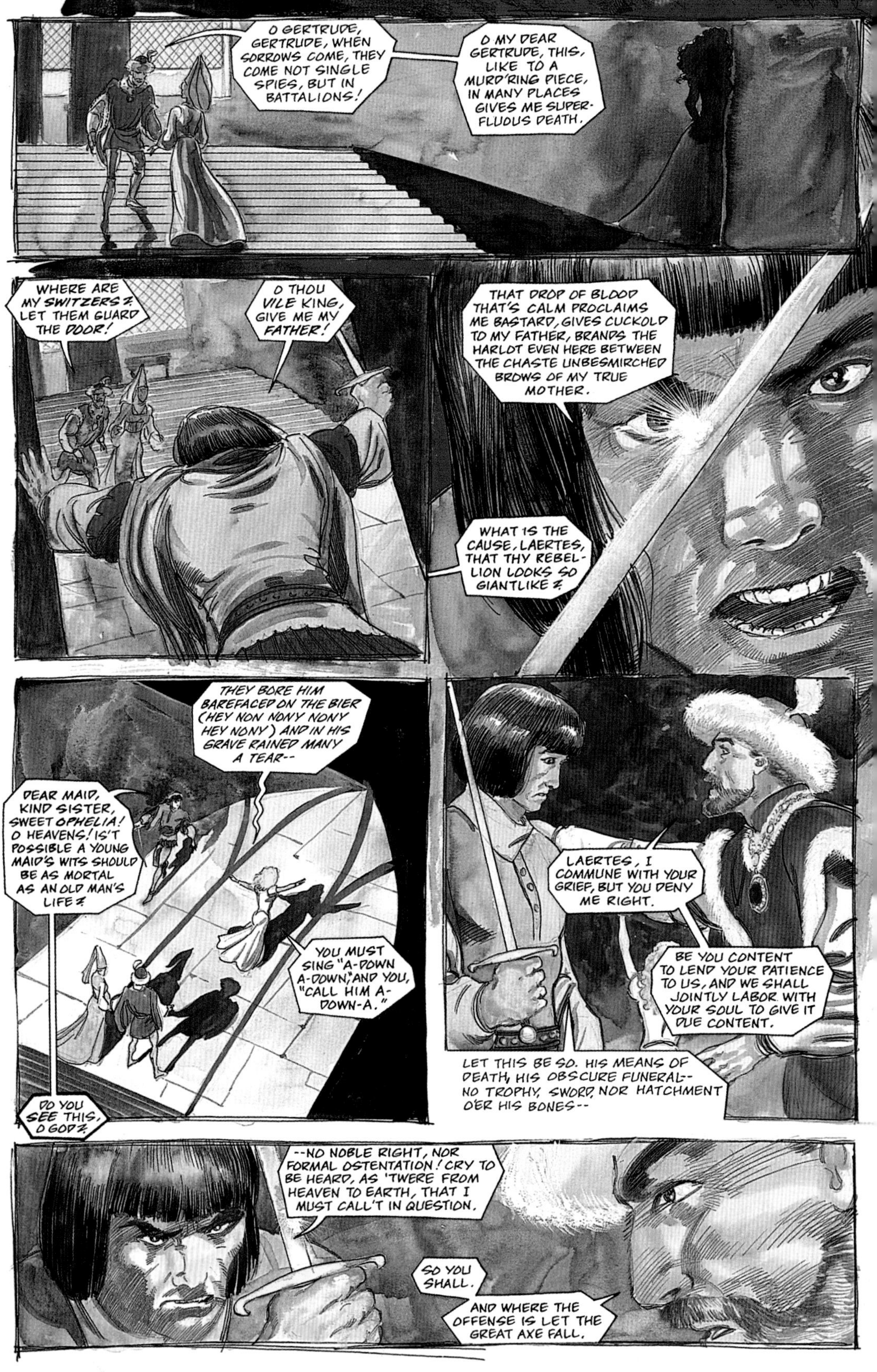
O GERTRUDE, GERTRUDE, WHEN SORROWS COME, THEY COME NOT SINGLE SPIES, BUT IN BATTALIONS!
O MY DEAR GERTRUDE, THIS, LIKE TO A MURD'RING PIECE, IN MANY PLACES GIVES ME SUPERFLUOUS DEATH.
WHERE ARE MY SWITZERS? LET THEM GUARD THE DOOR!
O THOU VILE KING, GIVE ME MY FATHER!
THAT DROP OF BLOOD THAT'S CALM PROCLAIMS ME BASTARD, GIVES CUCKOLD TO MY FATHER, BRANDS THE HARLOT EVEN HERE BETWEEN THE CHASTE UNBESMIRCHED BROWS OF MY TRUE MOTHER.
WHAT IS THE CAUSE, LAERTES, THAT THY REBELLION LOOKS SO GIANTLIKE?
THEY BORE HIM BAREFACED ON THE BIER (HEY NON NONY NONY HEY NONY) AND IN HIS GRAVE RAINED MANY A TEAR--
DEAR MAID, KIND SISTER, SWEET OPHELIA! O HEAVENS! IS'T POSSIBLE A YOUNG MAID'S WITS SHOULD BE AS MORTAL AS AN OLD MAN'S LIFE?
YOU MUST SING "A-DOWN A-DOWN," AND YOU, "CALL HIM A-DOWN-A."
DO YOU SEE THIS, O GOD?
LAERTES, I COMMUNE WITH YOUR GRIEF, BUT YOU DENY ME RIGHT.
BE YOU CONTENT TO LEND YOUR PATIENCE TO US, AND WE SHALL JOINTLY LABOR WITH YOUR SOUL TO GIVE IT DUE CONTENT.
LET THIS BE SO. HIS MEANS OF DEATH, HIS OBSCURE FUNERAL-- NO TROPHY, SWORD, NOR HATCHMENT O'ER HIS BONES--
--NO NOBLE RIGHT, NOR FORMAL OSTENTATION! CRY TO BE HEARD, AS 'TWERE FROM HEAVEN TO EARTH, THAT I MUST CALL'T IN QUESTION.
SO YOU SHALL.
AND WHERE THE OFFENSE IS LET THE GREAT AXE FALL.

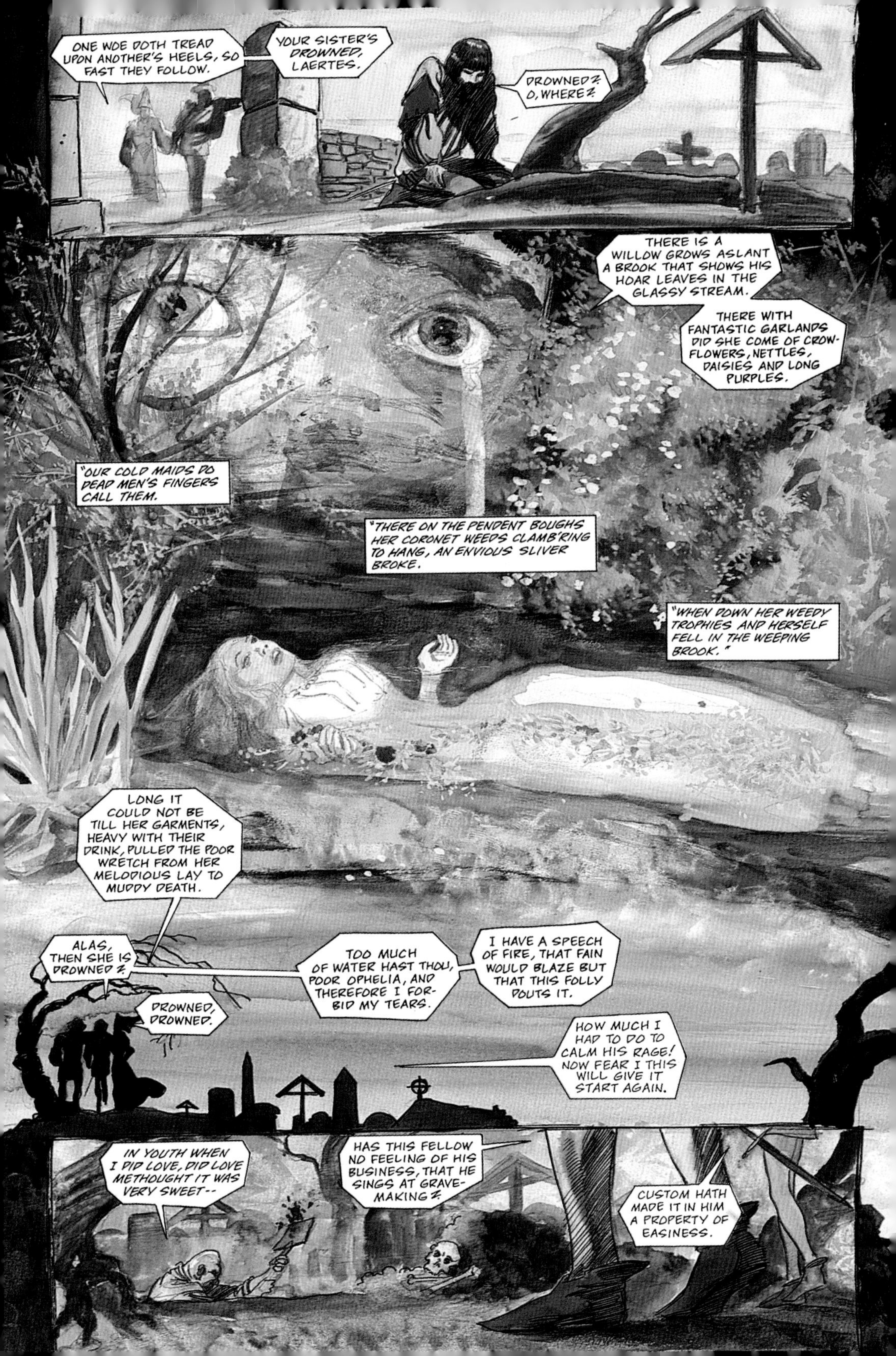
ONE WOE DOTH TREAD UPON ANOTHER'S HEELS, SO FAST THEY FOLLOW.
YOUR SISTER'S DROWNED, LAERTES.
DROWNED? O, WHERE?
THERE IS A WILLOW GROWS ASLANT A BROOK THAT SHOWS HIS HOAR LEAVES IN THE GLASSY STREAM.
THERE WITH FANTASTIC GARLANDS DID SHE COME OF CROW-FLOWERS, NETTLES, DAISIES AND LONG PURPLES.
"OUR COLD MAIDS DO DEAD MEN'S FINGERS CALL THEM.
"THERE ON THE PENDENT BOUGHS HER CORONET WEEDS CLAMB'RING TO HANG, AN ENVIOUS SLIVER BROKE.
"WHEN DOWN HER WEEDY TROPHIES AND HERSELF FELL IN THE WEEPING BROOK."
LONG IT COULD NOT BE TILL HER GARMENTS, HEAVY WITH THEIR DRINK, PULLED THE POOR WRETCH FROM HER MELODIOUS LAY TO MUDDY DEATH.
ALAS, THEN SHE IS DROWNED?
DROWNED, DROWNED.
TOO MUCH OF WATER HAST THOU, POOR OPHELIA, AND THEREFORE I FORBID MY TEARS.
I HAVE A SPEECH OF FIRE, THAT FAIN WOULD BLAZE BUT THAT THIS FOLLY DOUTS IT.
HOW MUCH I HAD TO DO TO CALM HIS RAGE! NOW FEAR I THIS WILL GIVE IT START AGAIN.
IN YOUTH WHEN I DID LOVE, DID LOVE METHOUGHT IT WAS VERY SWEET--
HAS THIS FELLOW NO FEELING OF HIS BUSINESS, THAT HE SINGS AT GRAVE-MAKING?
CUSTOM HATH MADE IT IN HIM A PROPERTY OF EASINESS.

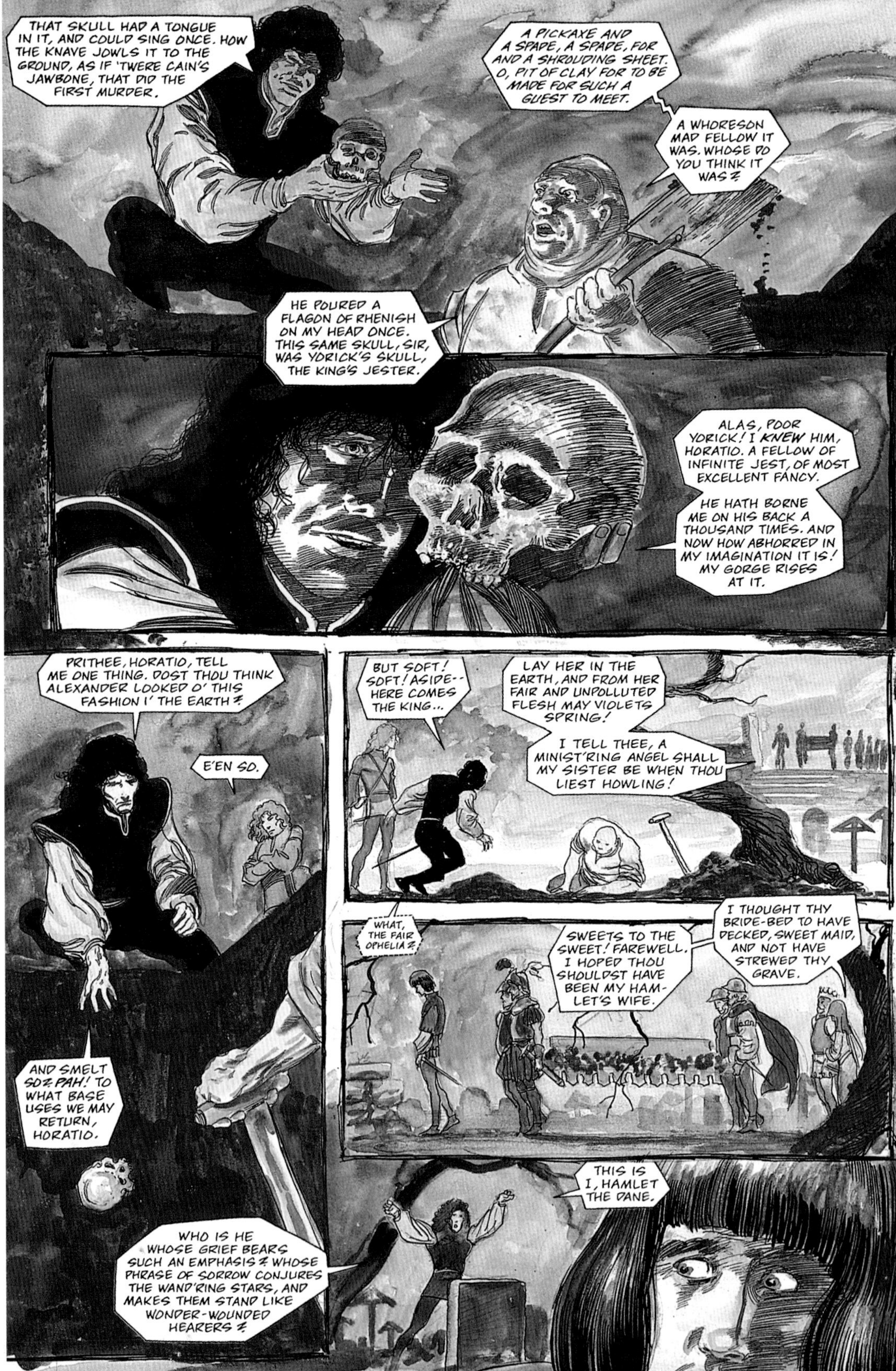
THAT SKULL HAD A TONGUE IN IT, AND COULD SING ONCE. HOW THE KNAVE JOWLS IT TO THE GROUND, AS IF 'TWERE CAIN'S JAWBONE, THAT DID THE FIRST MURDER.
A PICKAXE AND A SPADE, A SPADE, FOR AND A SHROUDING SHEET. O, PIT OF CLAY FOR TO BE MADE FOR SUCH A GUEST TO MEET.
A WHORESON MAD FELLOW IT WAS. WHOSE DO YOU THINK IT WAS?
HE POURED A FLAGON OF RHENISH ON MY HEAD ONCE. THIS SAME SKULL, SIR, WAS YORICK'S SKULL, THE KING'S JESTER.
ALAS, POOR YORICK! I KNEW HIM, HORATIO. A FELLOW OF INFINITE JEST, OF MOST EXCELLENT FANCY.
HE HATH BORNE ME ON HIS BACK A THOUSAND TIMES. AND NOW HOW ABHORRED IN MY IMAGINATION IT IS! MY GORGE RISES AT IT.
PRITHEE, HORATIO, TELL ME ONE THING. DOST THOU THINK ALEXANDER LOOKED O' THIS FASHION I' THE EARTH?
E'EN SO.
AND SMELT SO? PAH! TO WHAT BASE USES WE MAY RETURN, HORATIO.
BUT SOFT! SOFT! ASIDE-- HERE COMES THE KING...
LAY HER IN THE EARTH, AND FROM HER FAIR AND UNPOLLUTED FLESH MAY VIOLETS SPRING!
I TELL THEE, A MINIST'RING ANGEL SHALL MY SISTER BE WHEN THOU LIEST HOWLING!
WHAT, THE FAIR OPHELIA?
SWEETS TO THE SWEET! FAREWELL. I HOPED THOU SHOULDST HAVE BEEN MY HAMLET'S WIFE.
I THOUGHT THY BRIDE-BED TO HAVE DECKED, SWEET MAID, AND NOT HAVE STREWED THY GRAVE.
WHO IS HE WHOSE GRIEF BEARS SUCH AN EMPHASIS? WHOSE PHRASE OF SORROW CONJURES THE WAND'RING STARS, AND MAKES THEM STAND LIKE WONDER-WOUNDED HEARERS?
THIS IS I, HAMLET THE DANE.

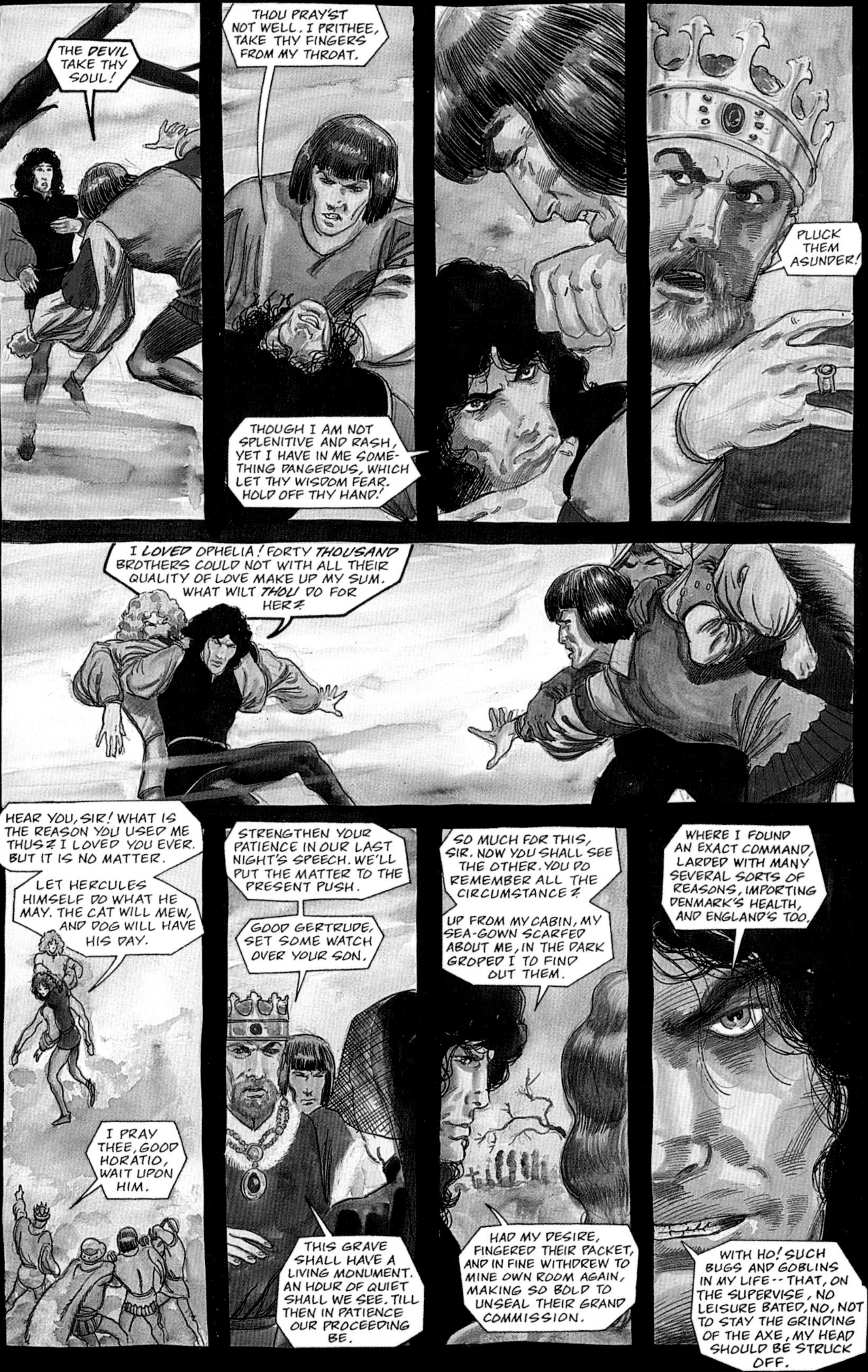
THE DEVIL TAKE THY SOUL!
THOU PRAY'ST NOT WELL. I PRITHEE, TAKE THY FINGERS FROM MY THROAT.
THOUGH I AM NOT SPLENITIVE AND RASH, YET I HAVE IN ME SOME-THING DANGEROUS, WHICH LET THY WISDOM FEAR. HOLD OFF THY HAND!
PLUCK THEM ASUNDER!
I LOVED OPHELIA! FORTY THOUSAND BROTHERS COULD NOT WITH ALL THEIR QUALITY OF LOVE MAKE UP MY SUM. WHAT WILT THOU DO FOR HER?
HEAR YOU, SIR! WHAT IS THE REASON YOU USED ME THUS? I LOVED YOU EVER. BUT IT IS NO MATTER.
LET HERCULES HIMSELF DO WHAT HE MAY. THE CAT WILL MEW, AND DOG WILL HAVE HIS DAY.
I PRAY THEE, GOOD HORATIO, WAIT UPON HIM.
STRENGTHEN YOUR PATIENCE IN OUR LAST NIGHT'S SPEECH. WE'LL PUT THE MATTER TO THE PRESENT PUSH.
GOOD GERTRUDE, SET SOME WATCH OVER YOUR SON.
THIS GRAVE SHALL HAVE A LIVING MONUMENT. AN HOUR OF QUIET SHALL WE SEE. TILL THEN IN PATIENCE OUR PROCEEDING BE.
SO MUCH FOR THIS, SIR. NOW YOU SHALL SEE THE OTHER. YOU DO REMEMBER ALL THE CIRCUMSTANCE?
UP FROM MY CABIN, MY SEA-GOWN SCARFED ABOUT ME, IN THE DARK GROPED I TO FIND OUT THEM.
HAD MY DESIRE, FINGERED THEIR PACKET, AND IN FINE WITHDREW TO MINE OWN ROOM AGAIN, MAKING SO BOLD TO UNSEAL THEIR GRAND COMMISSION.
WHERE I FOUND AN EXACT COMMAND, LARDED WITH MANY SEVERAL SORTS OF REASONS, IMPORTING DENMARK'S HEALTH, AND ENGLAND'S TOO.
WITH HO! SUCH BUGS AND GOBLINS IN MY LIFE -- THAT, ON THE SUPERVISE, NO LEISURE BATED, NO, NOT TO STAY THE GRINDING OF THE AXE, MY HEAD SHOULD BE STRUCK OFF.

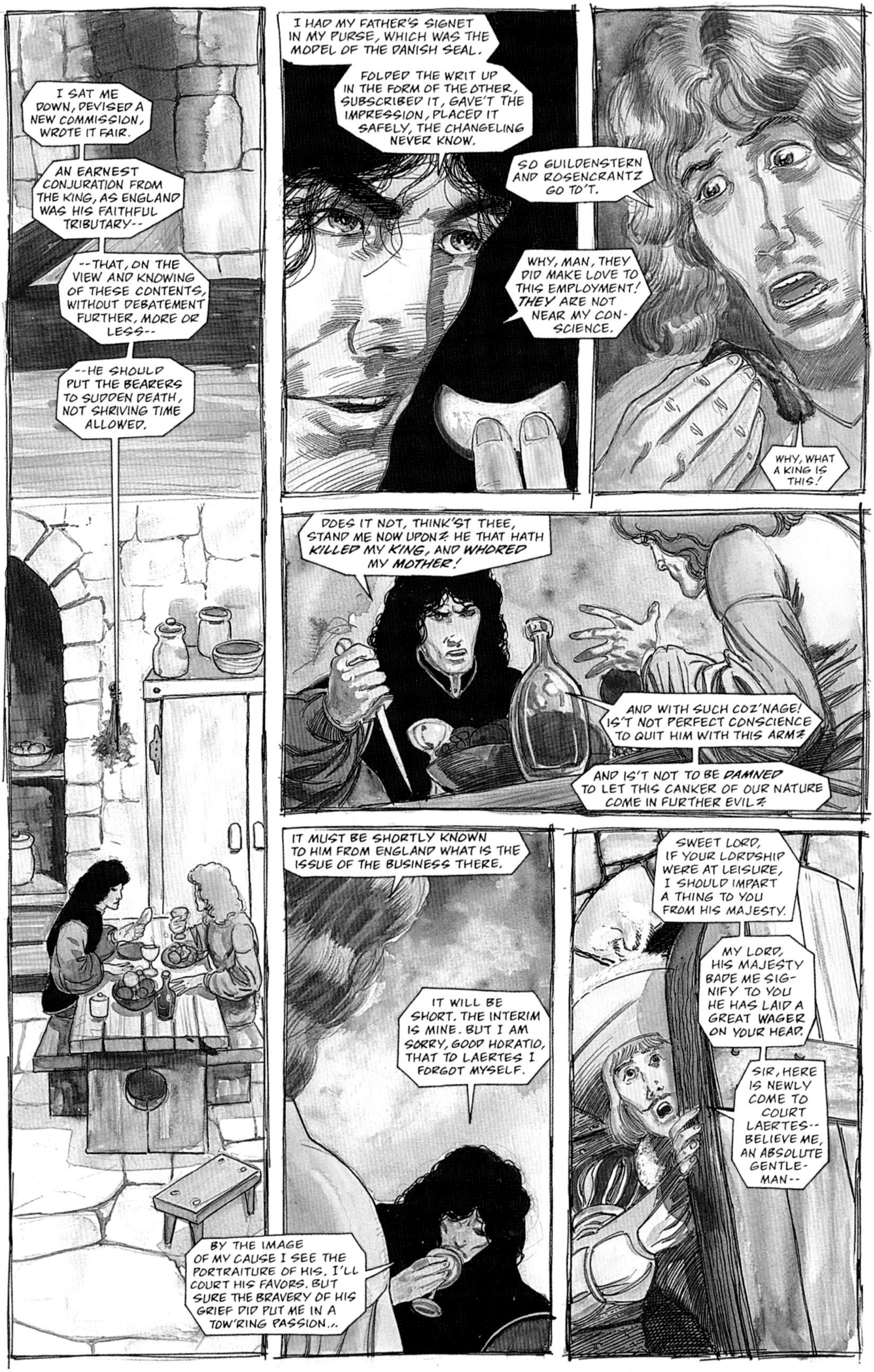
I SAT ME DOWN, DEVISED A NEW COMMISSION, WROTE IT FAIR.
AN EARNEST CONJURATION FROM THE KING, AS ENGLAND WAS HIS FAITHFUL TRIBUTARY--
--THAT, ON THE VIEW AND KNOWING OF THESE CONTENTS, WITHOUT DEBATEMENT FURTHER, MORE OR LESS--
--HE SHOULD PUT THE BEARERS TO SUDDEN DEATH, NOT SHRIVING TIME ALLOWED.
I HAD MY FATHER'S SIGNET IN MY PURSE, WHICH WAS THE MODEL OF THE DANISH SEAL.
FOLDED THE WRIT UP IN THE FORM OF THE OTHER, SUBSCRIBED IT, GAVE'T THE IMPRESSION, PLACED IT SAFELY, THE CHANGELING NEVER KNOW.
SO GUILDENSTERN AND ROSENCRANTZ GO TO'T.
WHY, MAN, THEY DID MAKE LOVE TO THIS EMPLOYMENT! THEY ARE NOT NEAR MY CONSCIENCE.
WHY, WHAT A KING IS THIS!
DOES IT NOT, THINK'ST THEE, STAND ME NOW UPON? HE THAT HATH KILLED MY KING, AND WHORED MY MOTHER!
AND WITH SUCH COZ'NAGE! IS'T NOT PERFECT CONSCIENCE TO QUIT HIM WITH THIS ARM?
AND IS'T NOT TO BE DAMNED TO LET THIS CANKER OF OUR NATURE COME IN FURTHER EVIL?
IT MUST BE SHORTLY KNOWN TO HIM FROM ENGLAND WHAT IS THE ISSUE OF THE BUSINESS THERE.
IT WILL BE SHORT. THE INTERIM IS MINE. BUT I AM SORRY, GOOD HORATIO, THAT TO LAERTES I FORGOT MYSELF.
BY THE IMAGE OF MY CAUSE I SEE THE PORTRAITURE OF HIS. I'LL COURT HIS FAVORS. BUT SURE THE BRAVERY OF HIS GRIEF DID PUT ME IN A TOW'RING PASSION...
SWEET LORD, IF YOUR LORDSHIP WERE AT LEISURE, I SHOULD IMPART A THING TO YOU FROM HIS MAJESTY.
MY LORD, HIS MAJESTY BADE ME SIGNIFY TO YOU HE HAS LAID A GREAT WAGER ON YOUR HEAD.
SIR, HERE IS NEWLY COME TO COURT LAERTES--BELIEVE ME, AN ABSOLUTE GENTLEMAN--

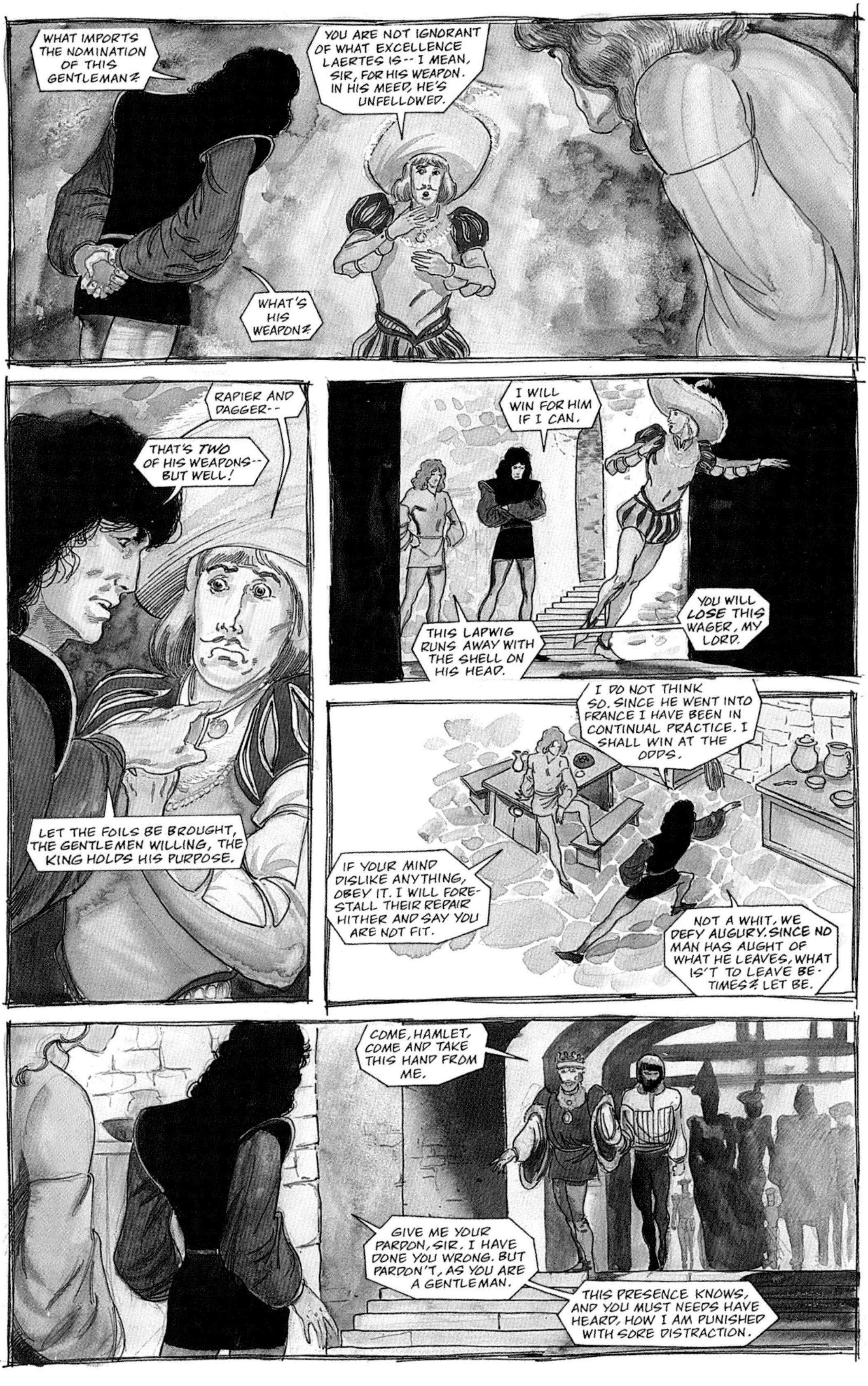
WHAT IMPORTS THE NOMINATION OF THIS GENTLEMAN?
YOU ARE NOT IGNORANT OF WHAT EXCELLENCE LAERTES IS -- I MEAN, SIR, FOR HIS WEAPON. IN HIS MEED, HE'S UNFELLOWED.
WHAT'S HIS WEAPON?
RAPIER AND DAGGER--
THAT'S *TWO* OF HIS WEAPONS-- BUT WELL!
LET THE FOILS BE BROUGHT, THE GENTLEMEN WILLING, THE KING HOLDS HIS PURPOSE.
I WILL WIN FOR HIM IF I CAN.
THIS LAPWIG RUNS AWAY WITH THE SHELL ON HIS HEAD.
YOU WILL *LOSE* THIS WAGER, MY LORD.
I DO NOT THINK SO. SINCE HE WENT INTO FRANCE I HAVE BEEN IN CONTINUAL PRACTICE. I SHALL WIN AT THE ODDS.
IF YOUR MIND DISLIKE ANYTHING, OBEY IT. I WILL FORE-STALL THEIR REPAIR HITHER AND SAY YOU ARE NOT FIT.
NOT A WHIT, WE DEFY AUGURY. SINCE NO MAN HAS AUGHT OF WHAT HE LEAVES, WHAT IS'T TO LEAVE BE-TIMES? LET BE.
COME, HAMLET, COME AND TAKE THIS HAND FROM ME.
GIVE ME YOUR PARDON, SIR. I HAVE DONE YOU WRONG. BUT PARDON'T, AS YOU ARE A GENTLEMAN.
THIS PRESENCE KNOWS, AND YOU MUST NEEDS HAVE HEARD, HOW I AM PUNISHED WITH SORE DISTRACTION.

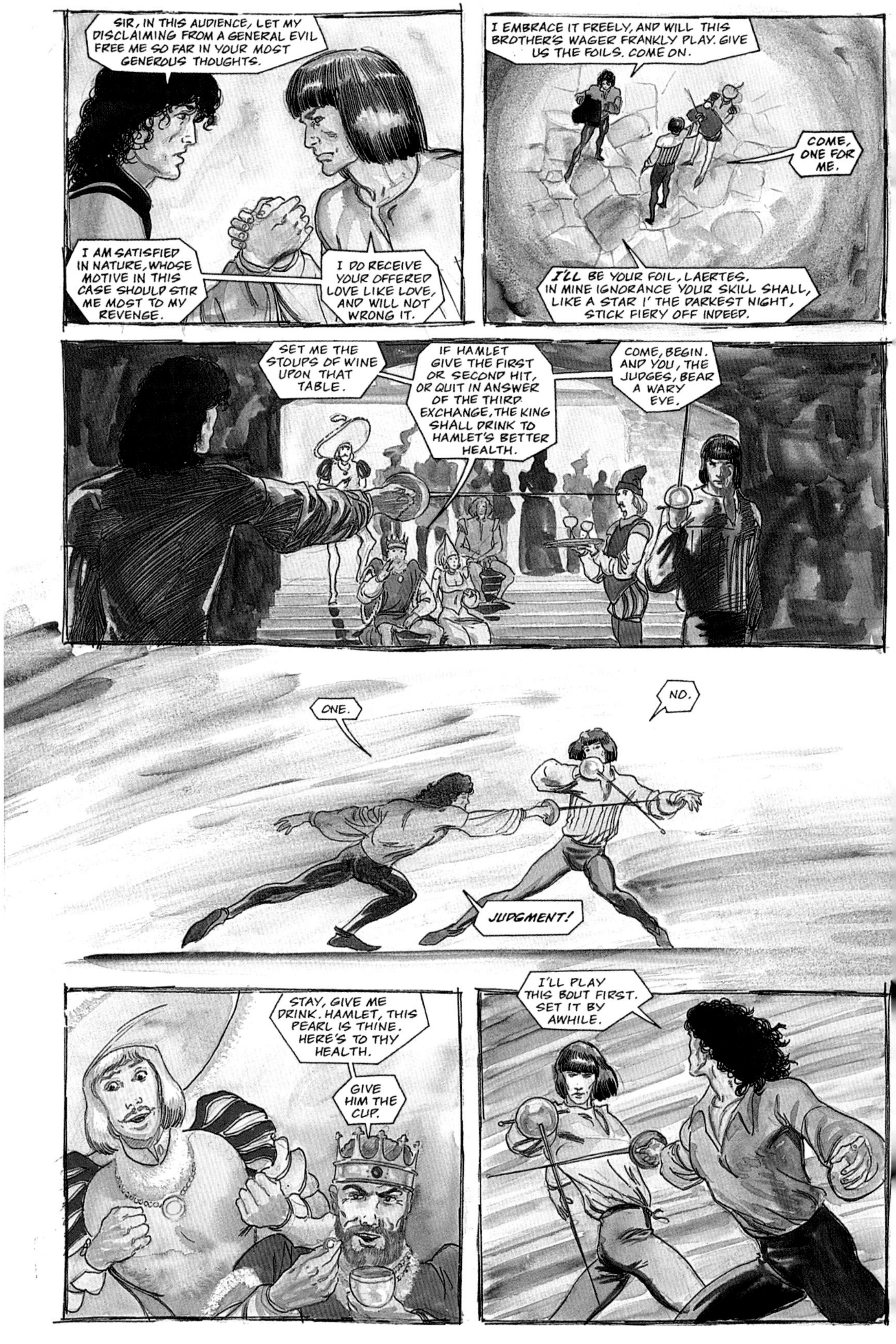
SIR, IN THIS AUDIENCE, LET MY DISCLAIMING FROM A GENERAL EVIL FREE ME SO FAR IN YOUR MOST GENEROUS THOUGHTS.
I AM SATISFIED IN NATURE, WHOSE MOTIVE IN THIS CASE SHOULD STIR ME MOST TO MY REVENGE.
I DO RECEIVE YOUR OFFERED LOVE LIKE LOVE, AND WILL NOT WRONG IT.
I EMBRACE IT FREELY, AND WILL THIS BROTHER'S WAGER FRANKLY PLAY. GIVE US THE FOILS. COME ON.
COME, ONE FOR ME.
I'LL BE YOUR FOIL, LAERTES. IN MINE IGNORANCE YOUR SKILL SHALL, LIKE A STAR I' THE DARKEST NIGHT, STICK FIERY OFF INDEED.
SET ME THE STOUPS OF WINE UPON THAT TABLE.
IF HAMLET GIVE THE FIRST OR SECOND HIT, OR QUIT IN ANSWER OF THE THIRD EXCHANGE, THE KING SHALL DRINK TO HAMLET'S BETTER HEALTH.
COME, BEGIN. AND YOU, THE JUDGES, BEAR A WARY EYE.
ONE.
NO.
JUDGMENT!
STAY, GIVE ME DRINK. HAMLET, THIS PEARL IS THINE. HERE'S TO THY HEALTH.
GIVE HIM THE CUP.
I'LL PLAY THIS BOUT FIRST. SET IT BY AWHILE.

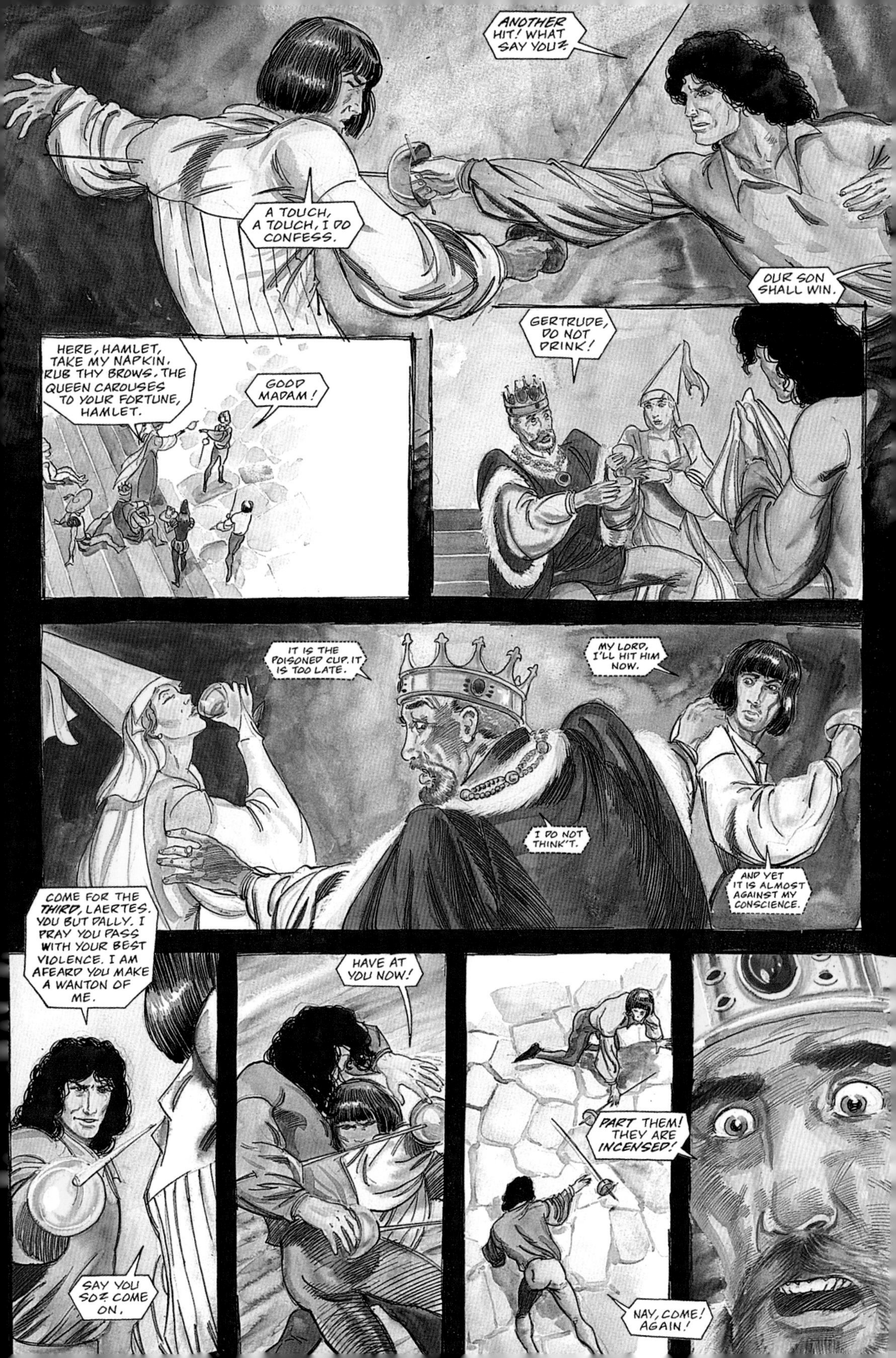

ANOTHER HIT! WHAT SAY YOU?
A TOUCH, A TOUCH, I DO CONFESS.
OUR SON SHALL WIN.
HERE, HAMLET, TAKE MY NAPKIN, RUB THY BROWS. THE QUEEN CAROUSES TO YOUR FORTUNE, HAMLET.
GOOD MADAM!
GERTRUDE, DO NOT DRINK!
IT IS THE POISONED CUP. IT IS TOO LATE.
MY LORD, I'LL HIT HIM NOW.
I DO NOT THINK'T.
AND YET IT IS ALMOST AGAINST MY CONSCIENCE.
COME FOR THE THIRD, LAERTES. YOU BUT DALLY. I PRAY YOU PASS WITH YOUR BEST VIOLENCE. I AM AFEARD YOU MAKE A WANTON OF ME.
SAY YOU SO? COME ON.
HAVE AT YOU NOW!
PART THEM! THEY ARE INCENSED!
NAY, COME! AGAIN!

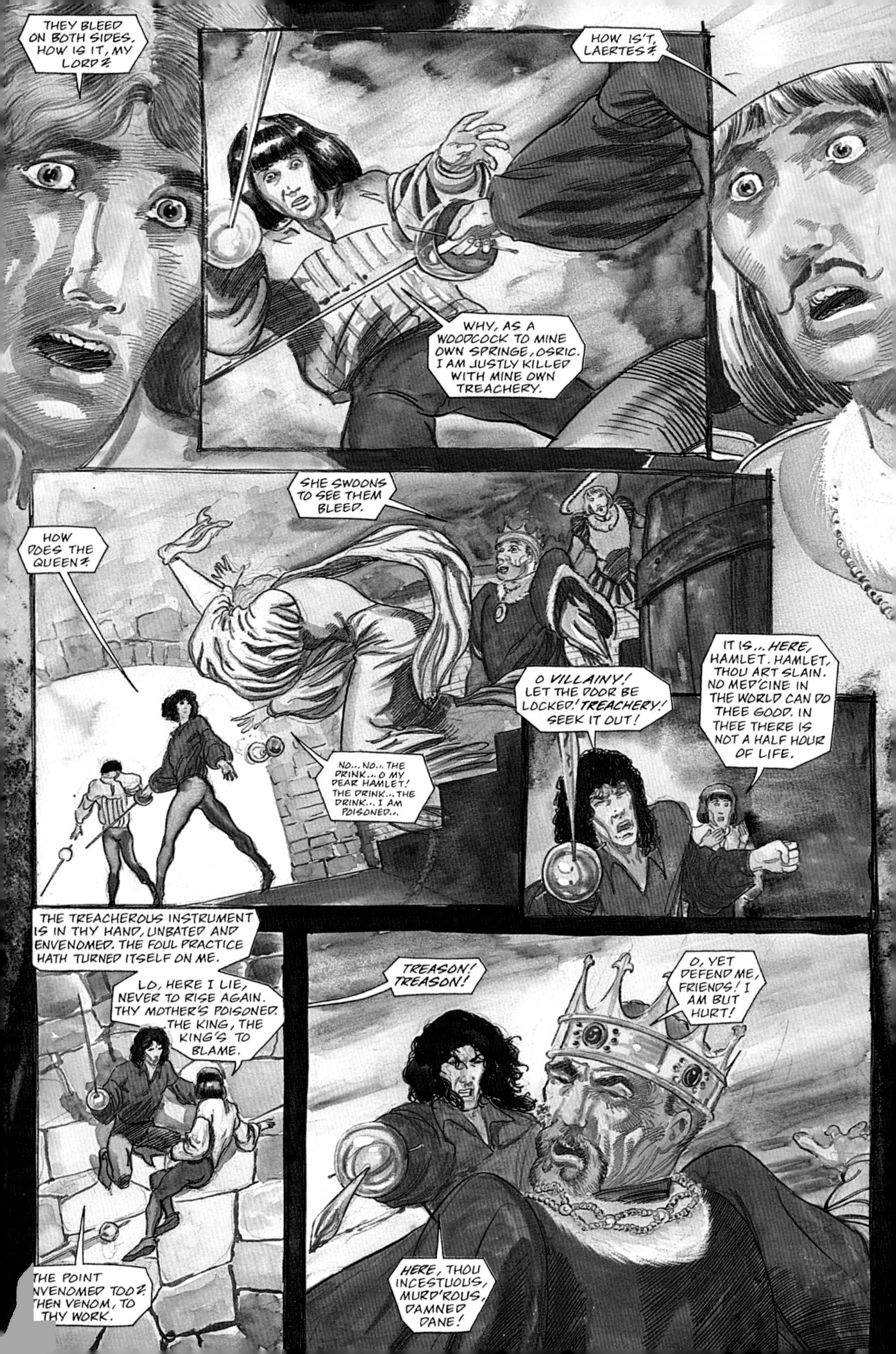
THEY BLEED ON BOTH SIDES. HOW IS IT, MY LORD?
HOW IS'T, LAERTES?
WHY, AS A WOODCOCK TO MINE OWN SPRINGE, OSRIC. I AM JUSTLY KILLED WITH MINE OWN TREACHERY.
SHE SWOONS TO SEE THEM BLEED.
HOW DOES THE QUEEN?
NO... NO... THE DRINK... O MY DEAR HAMLET! THE DRINK... THE DRINK... I AM POISONED...
O VILLAINY! LET THE DOOR BE LOCKED! TREACHERY! SEEK IT OUT!
IT IS... HERE, HAMLET. HAMLET, THOU ART SLAIN. NO MED'CINE IN THE WORLD CAN DO THEE GOOD. IN THEE THERE IS NOT A HALF HOUR OF LIFE.
THE TREACHEROUS INSTRUMENT IS IN THY HAND, UNBATED AND ENVENOMED. THE FOUL PRACTICE HATH TURNED ITSELF ON ME.
LO, HERE I LIE, NEVER TO RISE AGAIN. THY MOTHER'S POISONED. THE KING, THE KING'S TO BLAME.
THE POINT ENVENOMED TOO? THEN VENOM, TO THY WORK.
TREASON! TREASON!
O, YET DEFEND ME, FRIENDS! I AM BUT HURT!
HERE, THOU INCESTUOUS, MURD'ROUS, DAMNED DANE!

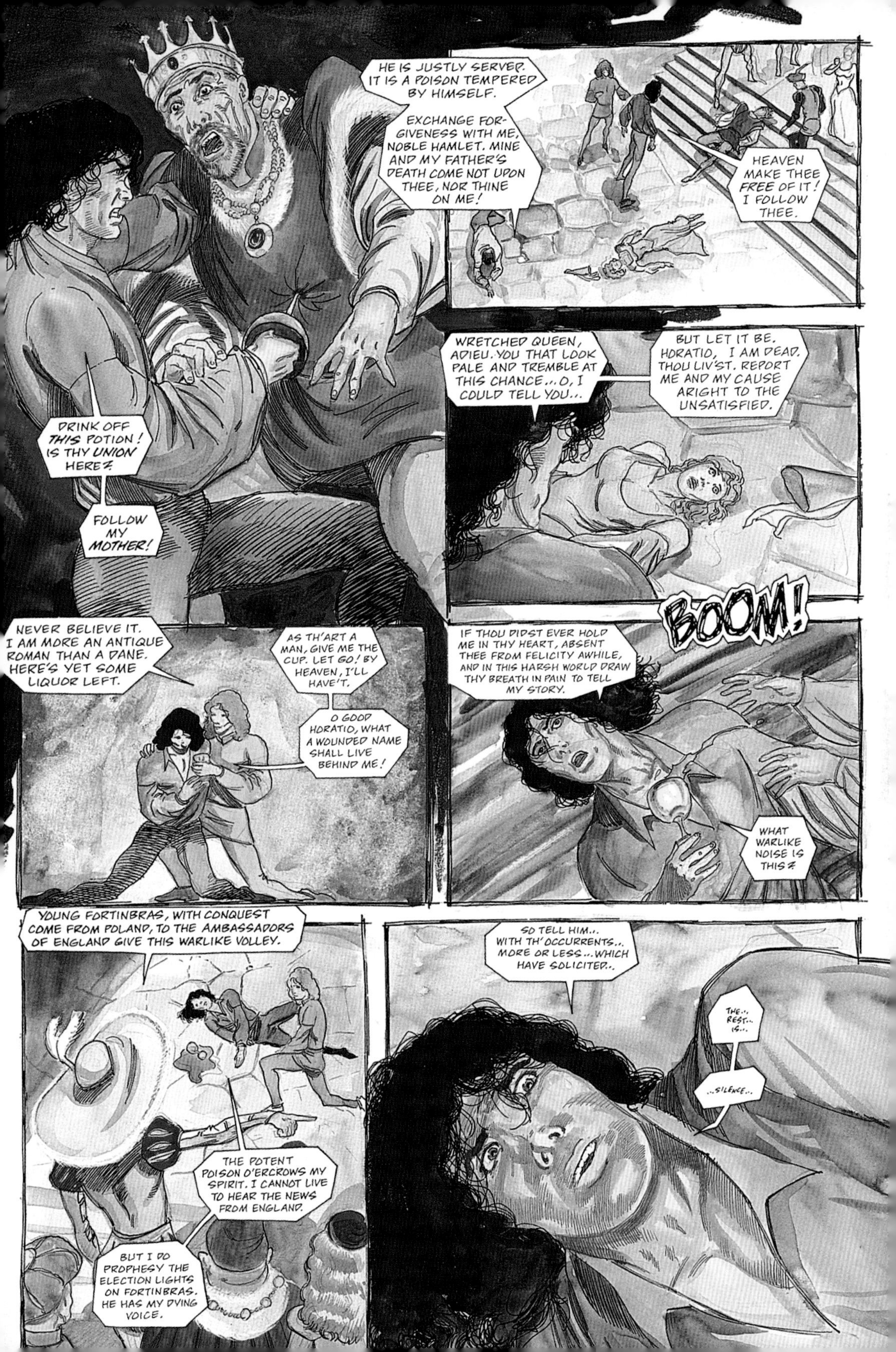
HE IS JUSTLY SERVED. IT IS A POISON TEMPERED BY HIMSELF.
EXCHANGE FORGIVENESS WITH ME, NOBLE HAMLET. MINE AND MY FATHER'S DEATH COME NOT UPON THEE, NOR THINE ON ME!
HEAVEN MAKE THEE FREE OF IT! I FOLLOW THEE.
DRINK OFF THIS POTION! IS THY UNION HERE?
FOLLOW MY MOTHER!
WRETCHED QUEEN, ADIEU. YOU THAT LOOK PALE AND TREMBLE AT THIS CHANCE... O, I COULD TELL YOU...
BUT LET IT BE. HORATIO, I AM DEAD. THOU LIV'ST. REPORT ME AND MY CAUSE ARIGHT TO THE UNSATISFIED.
NEVER BELIEVE IT. I AM MORE AN ANTIQUE ROMAN THAN A DANE. HERE'S YET SOME LIQUOR LEFT.
AS TH'ART A MAN, GIVE ME THE CUP. LET GO! BY HEAVEN, I'LL HAVE'T.
O GOOD HORATIO, WHAT A WOUNDED NAME SHALL LIVE BEHIND ME!
BOOM!
IF THOU DIDST EVER HOLD ME IN THY HEART, ABSENT THEE FROM FELICITY AWHILE, AND IN THIS HARSH WORLD DRAW THY BREATH IN PAIN TO TELL MY STORY.
WHAT WARLIKE NOISE IS THIS?
YOUNG FORTINBRAS, WITH CONQUEST COME FROM POLAND, TO THE AMBASSADORS OF ENGLAND GIVE THIS WARLIKE VOLLEY.
THE POTENT POISON O'ERCROWS MY SPIRIT. I CANNOT LIVE TO HEAR THE NEWS FROM ENGLAND.
BUT I DO PROPHESY THE ELECTION LIGHTS ON FORTINBRAS. HE HAS MY DYING VOICE.
SO TELL HIM... WITH TH'OCCURRENTS... MORE OR LESS... WHICH HAVE SOLICITED...
THE... REST... IS...
...SILENCE...

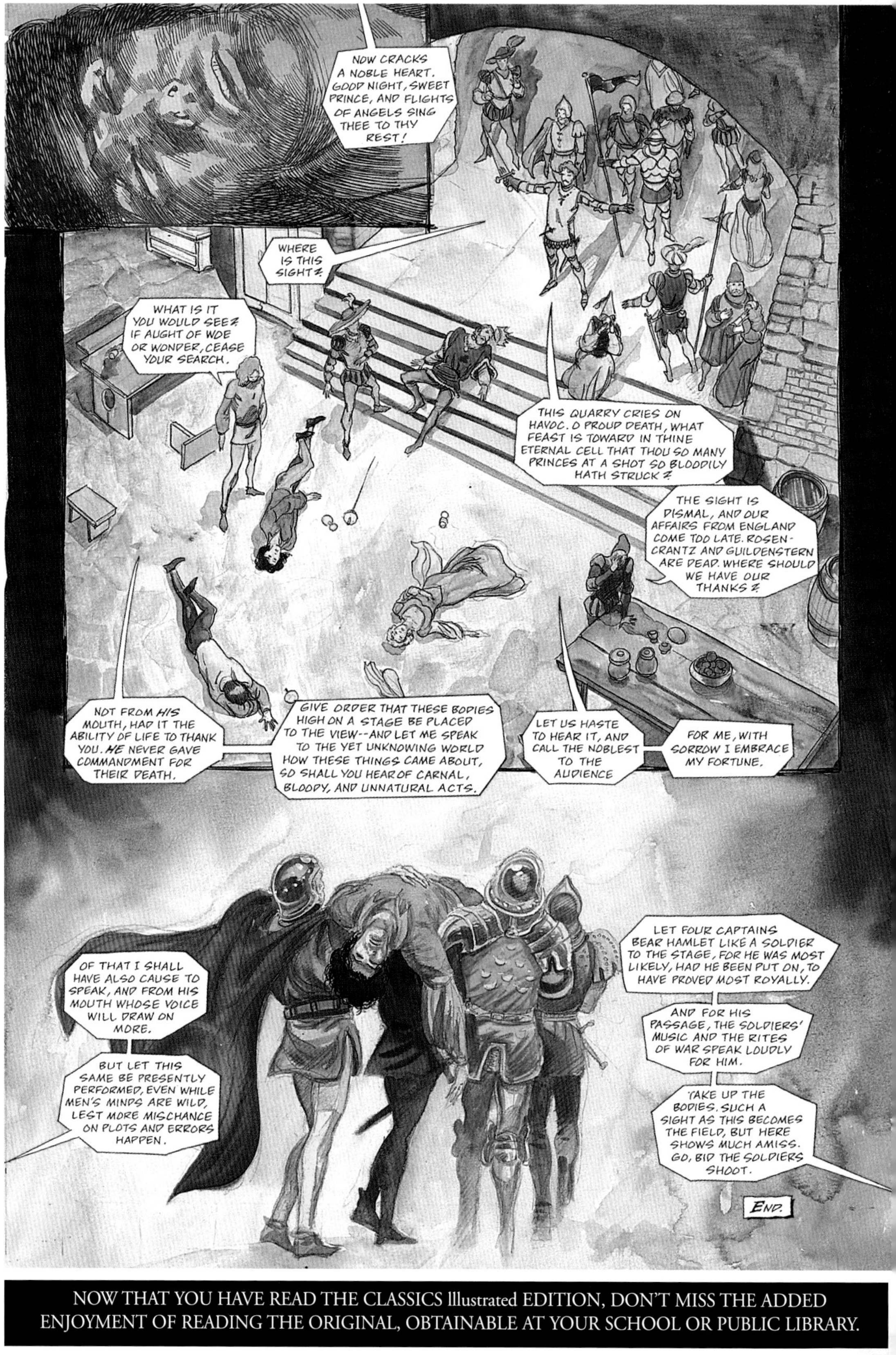
NOW CRACKS A NOBLE HEART. GOOD NIGHT, SWEET PRINCE, AND FLIGHTS OF ANGELS SING THEE TO THY REST!
WHERE IS THIS SIGHT?
WHAT IS IT YOU WOULD SEE? IF AUGHT OF WOE OR WONDER, CEASE YOUR SEARCH.
THIS QUARRY CRIES ON HAVOC. O PROUD DEATH, WHAT FEAST IS TOWARD IN THINE ETERNAL CELL THAT THOU SO MANY PRINCES AT A SHOT SO BLOODILY HATH STRUCK?
THE SIGHT IS DISMAL, AND OUR AFFAIRS FROM ENGLAND COME TOO LATE. ROSENCRANTZ AND GUILDENSTERN ARE DEAD. WHERE SHOULD WE HAVE OUR THANKS?
NOT FROM HIS MOUTH, HAD IT THE ABILITY OF LIFE TO THANK YOU. HE NEVER GAVE COMMANDMENT FOR THEIR DEATH.
GIVE ORDER THAT THESE BODIES HIGH ON A STAGE BE PLACED TO THE VIEW--AND LET ME SPEAK TO THE YET UNKNOWING WORLD HOW THESE THINGS CAME ABOUT, SO SHALL YOU HEAR OF CARNAL, BLOODY, AND UNNATURAL ACTS.
LET US HASTE TO HEAR IT, AND CALL THE NOBLEST TO THE AUDIENCE
FOR ME, WITH SORROW I EMBRACE MY FORTUNE.
OF THAT I SHALL HAVE ALSO CAUSE TO SPEAK, AND FROM HIS MOUTH WHOSE VOICE WILL DRAW ON MORE.
BUT LET THIS SAME BE PRESENTLY PERFORMED, EVEN WHILE MEN'S MINDS ARE WILD, LEST MORE MISCHANCE ON PLOTS AND ERRORS HAPPEN.
LET FOUR CAPTAINS BEAR HAMLET LIKE A SOLDIER TO THE STAGE, FOR HE WAS MOST LIKELY, HAD HE BEEN PUT ON, TO HAVE PROVED MOST ROYALLY.
AND FOR HIS PASSAGE, THE SOLDIERS' MUSIC AND THE RITES OF WAR SPEAK LOUDLY FOR HIM.
TAKE UP THE BODIES. SUCH A SIGHT AS THIS BECOMES THE FIELD, BUT HERE SHOWS MUCH AMISS. GO, BID THE SOLDIERS SHOOT.
END.

NOW THAT YOU HAVE READ THE CLASSICS Illustrated EDITION, DON'T MISS THE ADDED ENJOYMENT OF READING THE ORIGINAL, OBTAINABLE AT YOUR SCHOOL OR PUBLIC LIBRARY.

WATCH OUT FOR
PAPERCUTZ™

Welcome to the fifth edition of CLASSICS ILLUSTRATED. I'm Jim Salicrup, your humble and obedient Editor-in-Chief. This is what we call the Papercutz Backpages, where you find all the exciting developments happening with BIONICLE, THE HARDY BOYS, NANCY DREW, and TALES FROM THE CRYPT – but there's so much happening in the world of CLASSICS ILLUSTRATED, that we don't have enough room here. You'll need to go to www.papercutz.com for that! So, let's get right to it...

We've just gone back to press for the big second printing of CLASSICS ILLUS-TRATED #1 "Great Expectations" by Charles Dickens, adapted by Rick Geary! That's great news for you, as it's finally back in stock. *Newsweek* magazine noted the enormous creative challenge of fitting Dickens's novel into our limited page count — "It's a measure of Geary's talent that the story of the orphan Pip and his search for his anonymous benefactor still manages to read easily and swiftly..."

We also produced a special edition of CLASSICS ILLUSTRATED #2 "The Invisible Man" by H. G. Wells, adapted by Rick Geary for the Junior Library Guild. If your library or school is a subscriber, then you'll be able to borrow this special edition. Otherwise, the first printing is still available. For fans of Alan Moore's "League of Extraordinary Gentlemen," which featured the Invisible Man, be advised that we'll be publishing John K. Snyder III's adaptation of Robert Louis Stevenson's "Dr. Jekyll and Mr. Hyde" later this year.

Also flying off the shelves is Kyle Baker's adaptation of "Through the Looking-Glass" in CLASSICS ILLUSTRATED #3. Kyle's fans are making this one of our fastest-selling CLASSICS. Quickly catching up is CLASSICS ILLUS-TRATED #4 "The Raven and Other Poems" by Edgar Allan Poe, illustrated by Gahan Wilson, thanks to being released during April, which, as we all know, is Poetry Month. 2009 is also the 200th anniversary of the birth of Poe. *The New Yorker* magazine's Gahan Wilson's creepy cartoon illustrations only added to the overall macabre magnificence.

We're currently devouring *Classics Illustrated: A Cultural History* by William B. Jones Jr. It's the incredible story of the original CLASSICS ILLUSTRATED series, which was known for many years as "the largest juvenile publication in the world." We love this book, and think you will too. Don't forget that you can find full-color hardcover reproductions of many issues of the original series at www.jacklakeproductions.com .

Finally, on the following pages, we present an excerpt of Marion Mousse's adaptation of Mary Shelley's "Frankenstein" from CLASSICS ILLUSTRATED DELUXE #3. It's over twice as long as earlier adaptations, and we think it's a comic art masterpiece! Check it out...

Thanks,

Jim

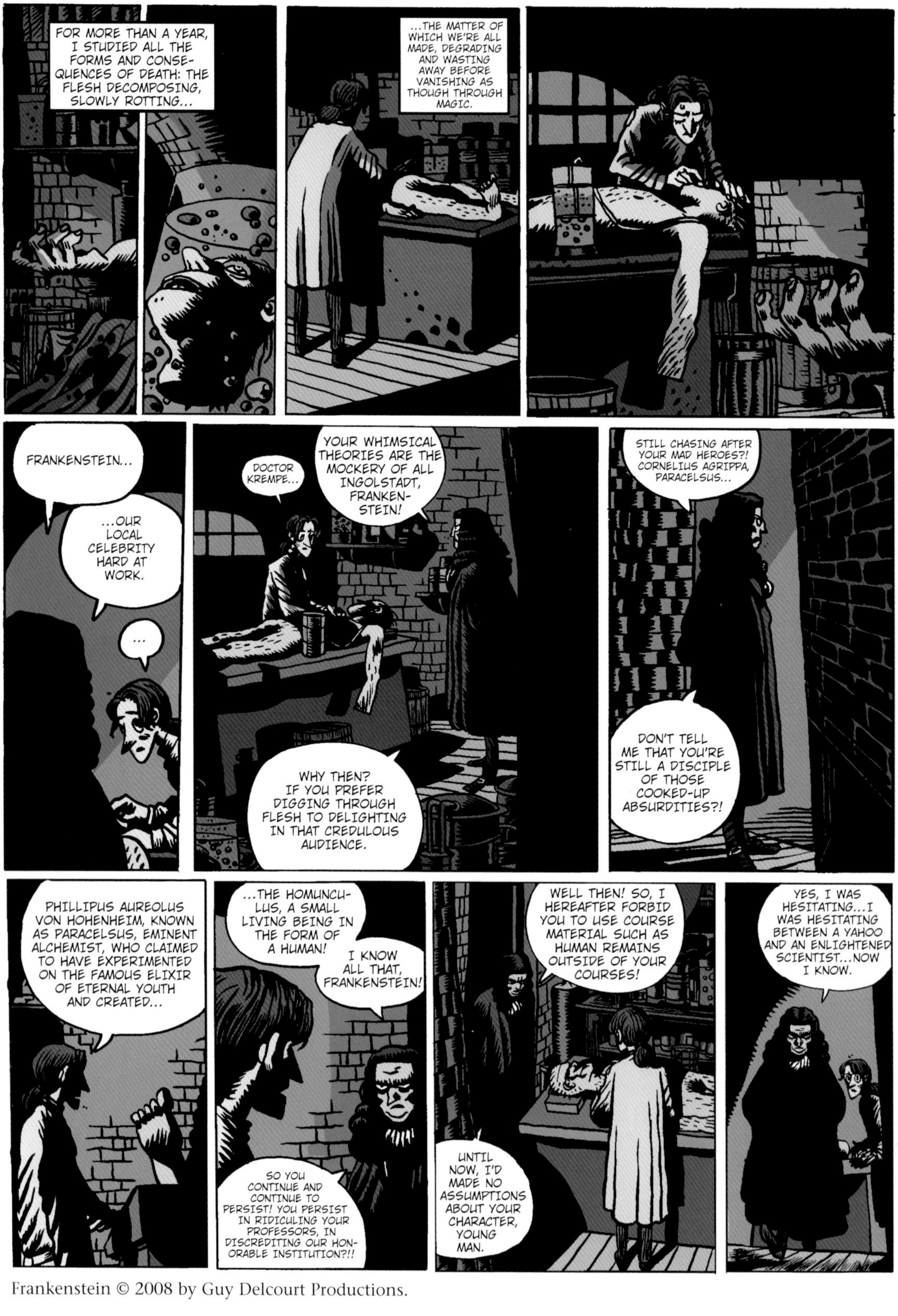
FOR MORE THAN A YEAR, I STUDIED ALL THE FORMS AND CONSE-QUENCES OF DEATH: THE FLESH DECOMPOSING, SLOWLY ROTTING...
...THE MATTER OF WHICH WE'RE ALL MADE, DEGRADING AND WASTING AWAY BEFORE VANISHING AS THOUGH THROUGH MAGIC.
FRANKENSTEIN...
...OUR LOCAL CELEBRITY HARD AT WORK.
...
DOCTOR KREMPE...
YOUR WHIMSICAL THEORIES ARE THE MOCKERY OF ALL INGOLSTADT, FRANKEN-STEIN!
WHY THEN? IF YOU PREFER DIGGING THROUGH FLESH TO DELIGHTING IN THAT CREDULOUS AUDIENCE.
STILL CHASING AFTER YOUR MAD HEROES?! CORNELIUS AGRIPPA, PARACELSUS...
DON'T TELL ME THAT YOU'RE STILL A DISCIPLE OF THOSE COOKED-UP ABSURDITIES?!
PHILLIPUS AUREOLUS VON HOHENHEIM, KNOWN AS PARACELSUS, EMINENT ALCHEMIST, WHO CLAIMED TO HAVE EXPERIMENTED ON THE FAMOUS ELIXIR OF ETERNAL YOUTH AND CREATED...
...THE HOMUNCU-LUS, A SMALL LIVING BEING IN THE FORM OF A HUMAN!
I KNOW ALL THAT, FRANKENSTEIN!
SO YOU CONTINUE AND CONTINUE TO PERSIST! YOU PERSIST IN RIDICULING YOUR PROFESSORS, IN DISCREDITING OUR HON-ORABLE INSTITUTION?!!
WELL THEN! SO, I HEREAFTER FORBID YOU TO USE COURSE MATERIAL SUCH AS HUMAN REMAINS OUTSIDE OF YOUR COURSES!
UNTIL NOW, I'D MADE NO ASSUMPTIONS ABOUT YOUR CHARACTER, YOUNG MAN.
YES, I WAS HESITATING...I WAS HESITATING BETWEEN A YAHOO AND AN ENLIGHTENED SCIENTIST...NOW I KNOW.

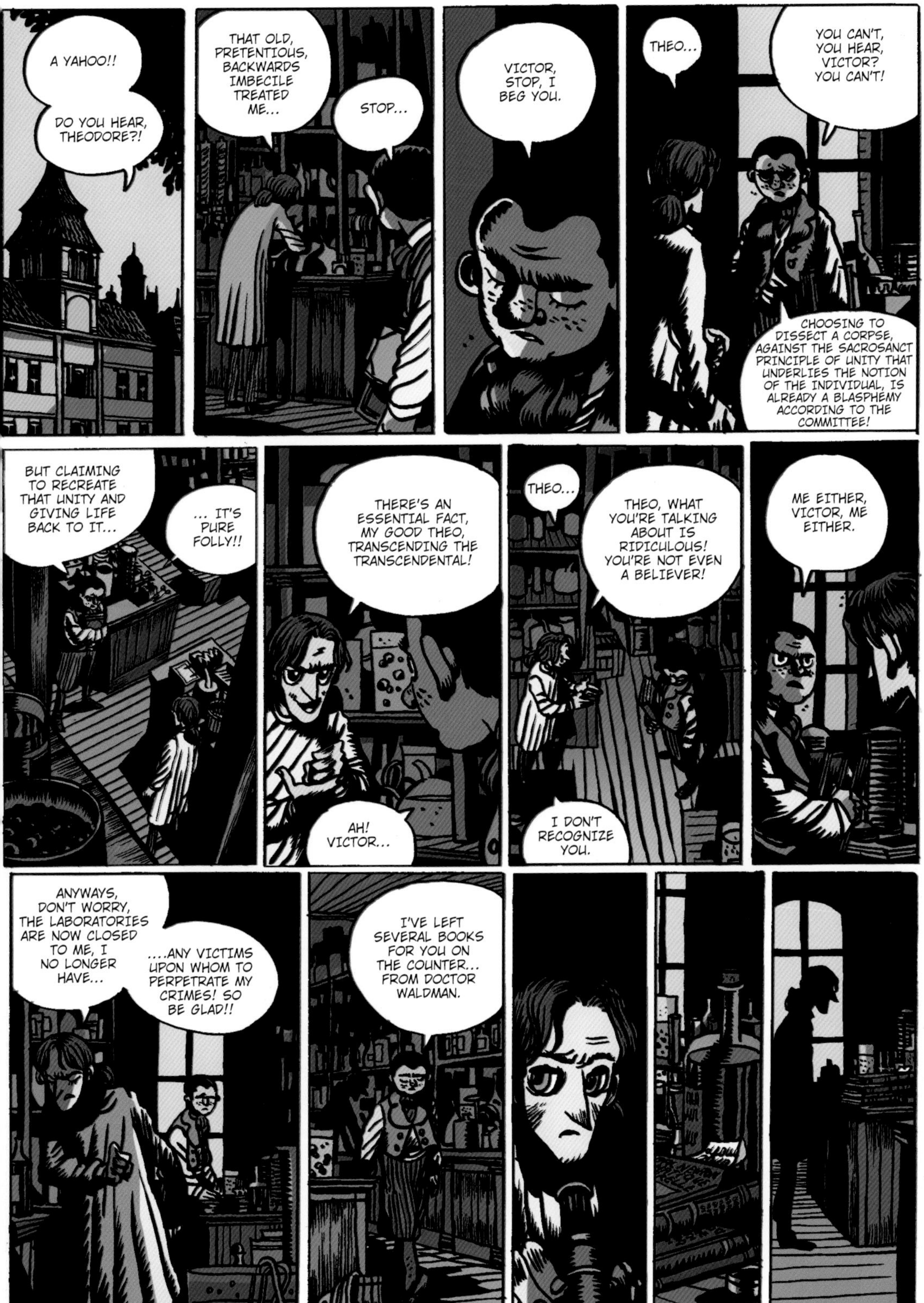
A YAHOO!!
DO YOU HEAR, THEODORE?!
THAT OLD, PRETENTIOUS, BACKWARDS IMBECILE TREATED ME...
STOP...
VICTOR, STOP, I BEG YOU.
THEO...
YOU CAN'T, YOU HEAR, VICTOR? YOU CAN'T!
CHOOSING TO DISSECT A CORPSE, AGAINST THE SACROSANCT PRINCIPLE OF UNITY THAT UNDERLIES THE NOTION OF THE INDIVIDUAL, IS ALREADY A BLASPHEMY ACCORDING TO THE COMMITTEE!
BUT CLAIMING TO RECREATE THAT UNITY AND GIVING LIFE BACK TO IT...
... IT'S PURE FOLLY!!
THERE'S AN ESSENTIAL FACT, MY GOOD THEO, TRANSCENDING THE TRANSCENDENTAL!
AH! VICTOR...
THEO...
THEO, WHAT YOU'RE TALKING ABOUT IS RIDICULOUS! YOU'RE NOT EVEN A BELIEVER!
I DON'T RECOGNIZE YOU.
ME EITHER, VICTOR, ME EITHER.
ANYWAYS, DON'T WORRY, THE LABORATORIES ARE NOW CLOSED TO ME, I NO LONGER HAVE...
....ANY VICTIMS UPON WHOM TO PERPETRATE MY CRIMES! SO BE GLAD!!
I'VE LEFT SEVERAL BOOKS FOR YOU ON THE COUNTER... FROM DOCTOR WALDMAN.

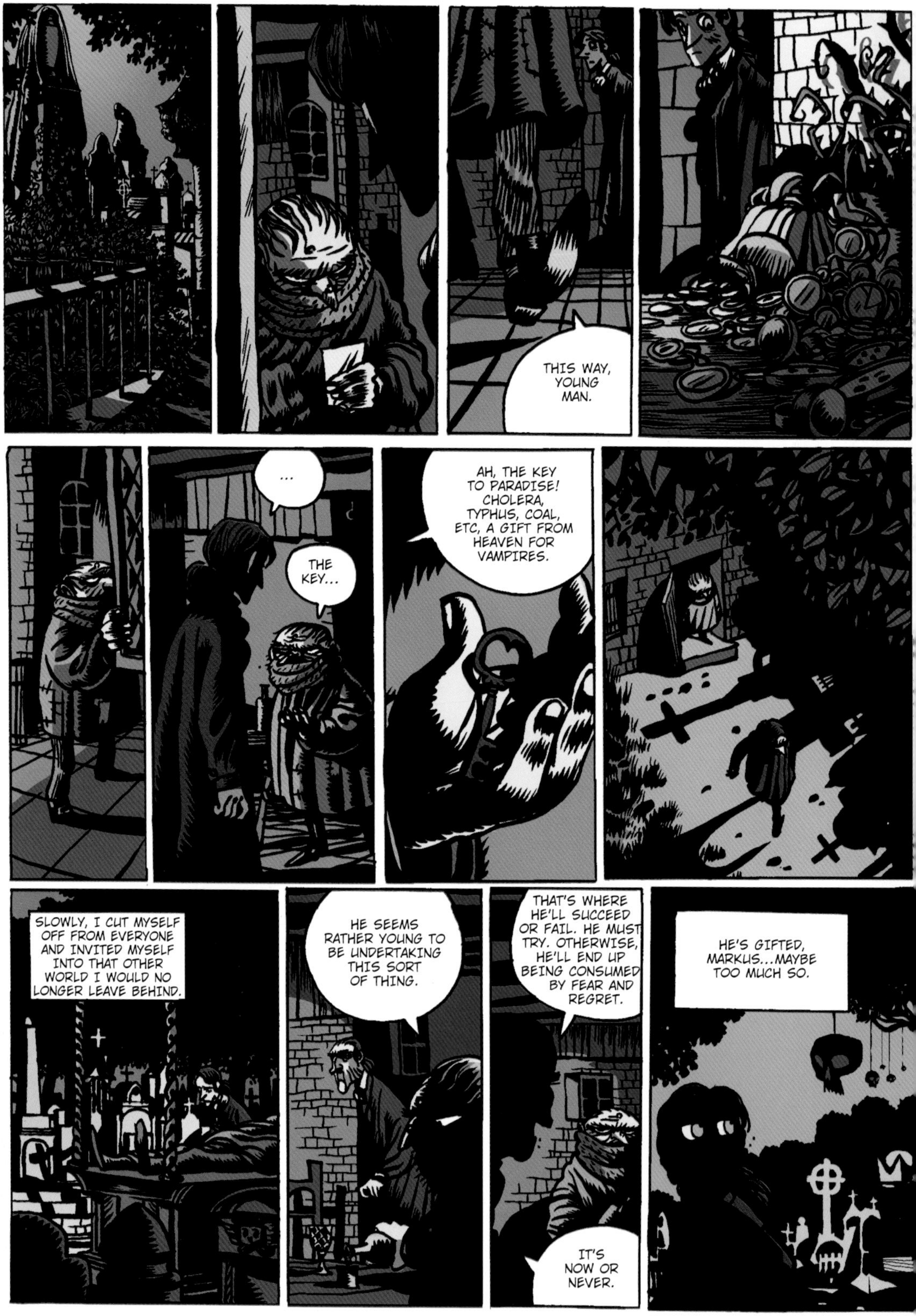
THIS WAY, YOUNG MAN.
...
THE KEY...
AH, THE KEY TO PARADISE! CHOLERA, TYPHUS, COAL, ETC, A GIFT FROM HEAVEN FOR VAMPIRES.
SLOWLY, I CUT MYSELF OFF FROM EVERYONE AND INVITED MYSELF INTO THAT OTHER WORLD I WOULD NO LONGER LEAVE BEHIND.
HE SEEMS RATHER YOUNG TO BE UNDERTAKING THIS SORT OF THING.
THAT'S WHERE HE'LL SUCCEED OR FAIL. HE MUST TRY. OTHERWISE, HE'LL END UP BEING CONSUMED BY FEAR AND REGRET.
IT'S NOW OR NEVER.
HE'S GIFTED, MARKUS...MAYBE TOO MUCH SO.

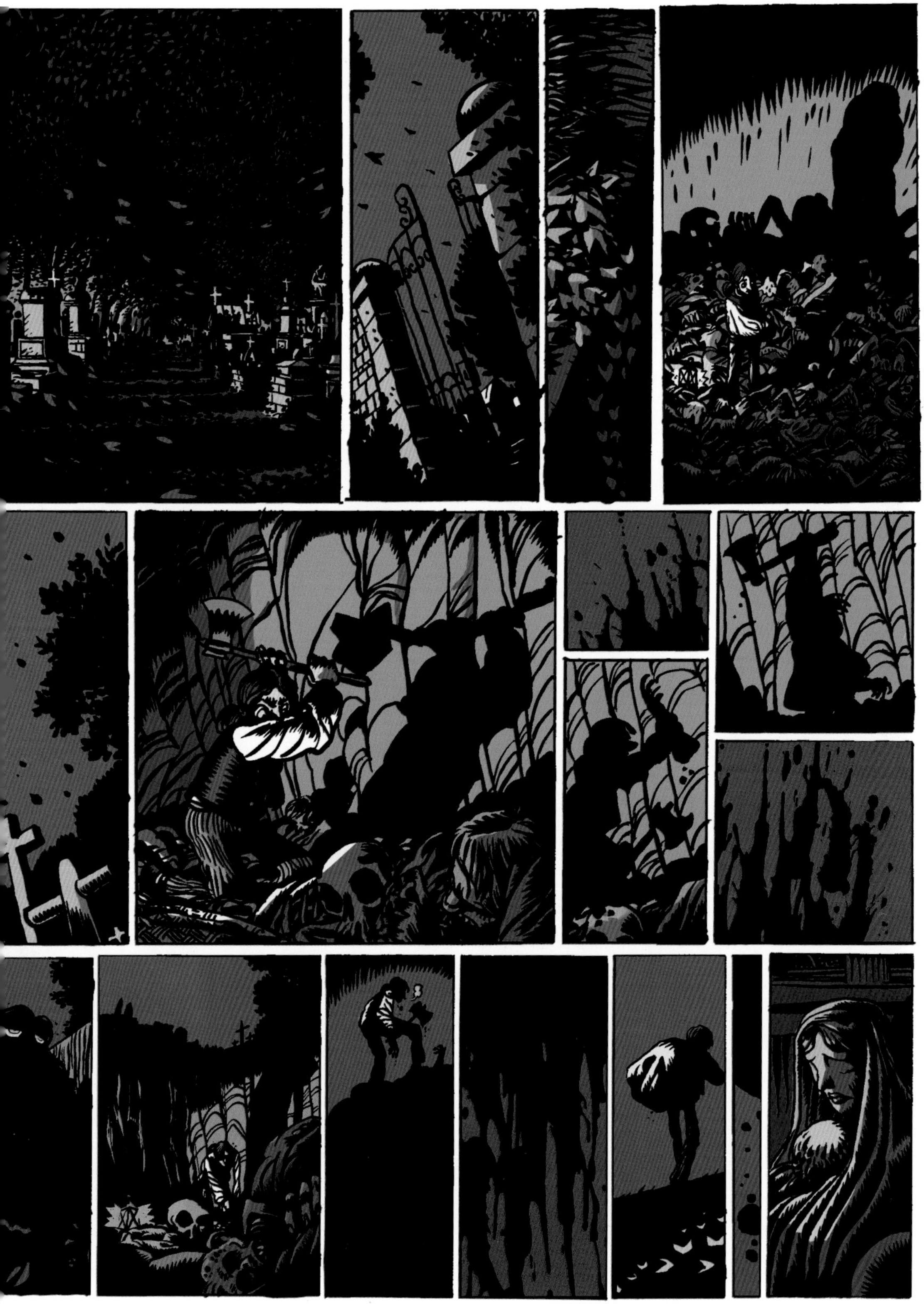

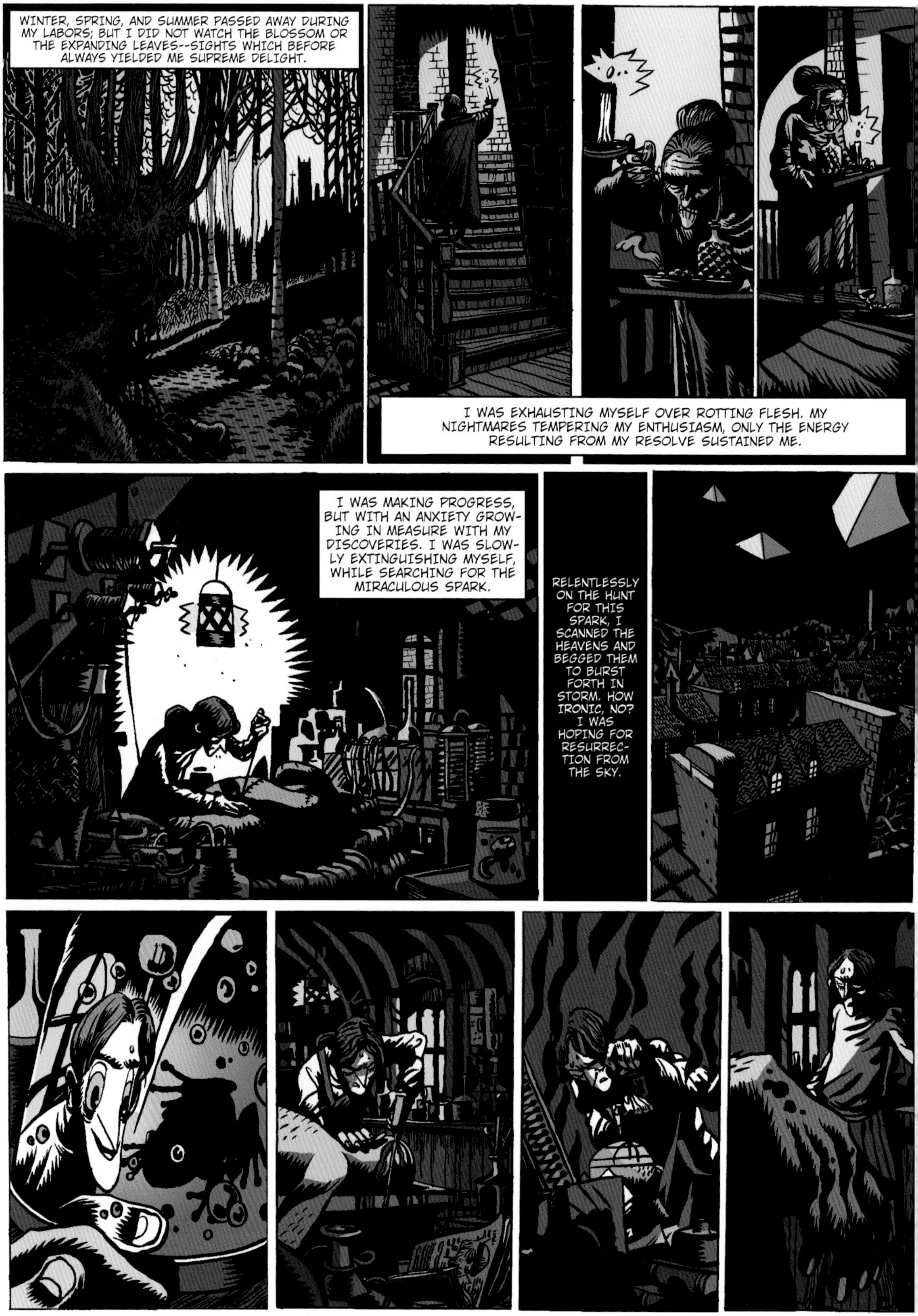
WINTER, SPRING, AND SUMMER PASSED AWAY DURING MY LABORS; BUT I DID NOT WATCH THE BLOSSOM OR THE EXPANDING LEAVES--SIGHTS WHICH BEFORE ALWAYS YIELDED ME SUPREME DELIGHT.
I WAS EXHAUSTING MYSELF OVER ROTTING FLESH. MY NIGHTMARES TEMPERING MY ENTHUSIASM, ONLY THE ENERGY RESULTING FROM MY RESOLVE SUSTAINED ME.
I WAS MAKING PROGRESS, BUT WITH AN ANXIETY GROWING IN MEASURE WITH MY DISCOVERIES. I WAS SLOWLY EXTINGUISHING MYSELF, WHILE SEARCHING FOR THE MIRACULOUS SPARK.
RELENTLESSLY ON THE HUNT FOR THIS SPARK, I SCANNED THE HEAVENS AND BEGGED THEM TO BURST FORTH IN STORM. HOW IRONIC, NO? I WAS HOPING FOR RESURRECTION FROM THE SKY.

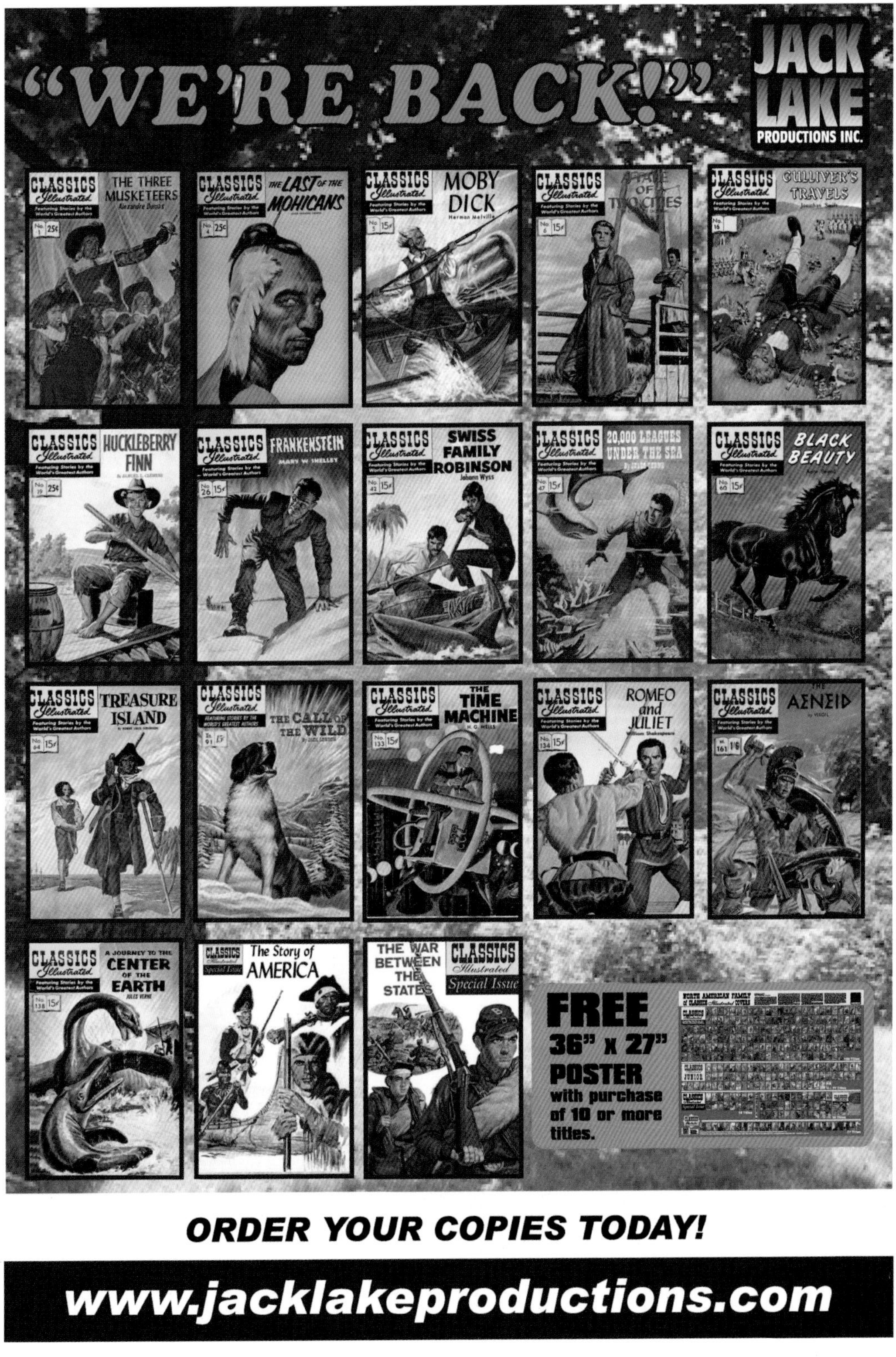
"WE'RE BACK!"
JACK LAKE PRODUCTIONS INC.
CLASSICS Illustrated THE THREE MUSKETEERS Alexandre Dumas
CLASSICS Illustrated THE LAST OF THE MOHICANS
CLASSICS Illustrated MOBY DICK Herman Melville
CLASSICS Illustrated A TALE OF TWO CITIES
CLASSICS Illustrated GULLIVER'S TRAVELS
CLASSICS Illustrated HUCKLEBERRY FINN
CLASSICS Illustrated FRANKENSTEIN MARY W. SHELLEY
CLASSICS Illustrated SWISS FAMILY ROBINSON Johann Wyss
CLASSICS Illustrated 20,000 LEAGUES UNDER THE SEA
CLASSICS Illustrated BLACK BEAUTY
CLASSICS Illustrated TREASURE ISLAND
CLASSICS Illustrated THE CALL OF THE WILD
CLASSICS Illustrated THE TIME MACHINE H.G. WELLS
CLASSICS Illustrated ROMEO and JULIET William Shakespeare
CLASSICS Illustrated THE AENEID
CLASSICS Illustrated A JOURNEY TO THE CENTER OF THE EARTH JULES VERNE
CLASSICS Illustrated Special Issue The Story of AMERICA
THE WAR BETWEEN THE STATES CLASSICS Illustrated Special Issue
FREE 36" x 27" POSTER with purchase of 10 or more titles.

SHAKESPEARE, MANDRAKE, & GRANT

William Shakespeare was baptized in Holy Trinity Church in Stratford-upon-Avon, England, on April 26, 1564. Since the prevailing custom was to christen children three days after birth, Shakespeare is presumed to have been born on April 23, 1564. The third of eight children, Shakespeare was the oldest son born to Mary Arden and John Shakespeare, a prominent shopkeeper who held several local elected offices. Almost nothing is known about Shakespeare's youth and early manhood; it is believed that he attended the local grammar school and then spent several years as a teacher. In 1582, Shakespeare married Anne Hathaway, who was eight years his senior. They had three children: Susanna, born in 1583, and Hamnet and Judith, twins born in 1585. In 1594, Shakespeare joined The Lord Chamberlain's Men London-based troupe as a leading member, and quickly established himself in the city's literary and theatrical community. His relationship with the company (later known as the King's Men) continued throughout his career; the troupe soon developed into London's leading company, occupying both the Globe and the Blackfriars theatres. It is difficult to tell when or in what order Shakespeare wrote his plays. Most scholars agree, though, that Shakespeare began writing for the stage in the late 1580's. His earliest plays apparently include *The Comedy of Errors*, the ambitious *Henry VI* trilogy, *Richard III, Richard II, The Taming of the Shrew*, and *Love's Labour's Lost*. Encouraged, perhaps, by the success of his light-hearted burlesques, Shakespeare then concentrated on a series of comedies, among them *A Midsummer Night's Dream, The Merchant of Venice, Much Ado About Nothing, As You Like It,* and *Twelfth Night*. In his later life, Shakespeare turned again to history and tragedy, composing such plays as *Romeo and Juliet, Henry IV Parts One and Two, Henry V, Julius Caesar, Hamlet, Othello, King Lear, Macbeth,* and *Antony and Cleopatra*. Interspersed among these were his *Sonnets*, and a few comedies and romantic tragic-comedies, such as *All's Well that Ends Well, Measure for Measure*, and *The Tempest*. With an income deriving from three sources - proceeds from the sale of his plays, his wages as an actor, and his share of the company's profits - Shakespeare prospered, enabling him to house his family in Stratford while he spent lengthy periods in London. Around 1611, he resettled in Stratford, retiring in 1613. Shakespeare died on April 23, 1616, and was buried in Holy Trinity Church. His works form the basis for the English theatrical tradition, and remain among the world's favorite plays.

Tom Mandrake was born in Ashtabula, Ohio, in 1956. He studied at the Cooper School of Art in Cleveland and the Joe Kubert School of Cartoon and Graphic Art in Dover, New Jersey, where he returned to co-develop the correspondence course in horror comics. His credits include *Batman, New Mutants, Captain Marvel, Justice League of America Destiny, Call of Duty: The Precinct, Animal Man, Creeps, The Spectre, Swamp Thing, Firestorm, the Spirit,* and *Grimjack*.

Steven Grant was born in Madison, Wisconsin, in 1953. He graduated from the University of Wisconsin, where he studied communication arts, and comparative mythology. Grant's comics credits include *Twilight Man, Whisper, Punisher, The Incredible Hulk,* and *The Avengers*. The former editor-in-chief of the *Velvet Light Trap Review of Cinema*, Grant has written music criticism for Trouser Press, and has contributed to several books on popular culture, including *Close-Ups and The Rock Yearbook*. Grant has also written a variety of widely praised young-adult adventure novels. He currently writes the column *Permanent Damage* as a staff writer for the online magazine *Comic Book Resources*.

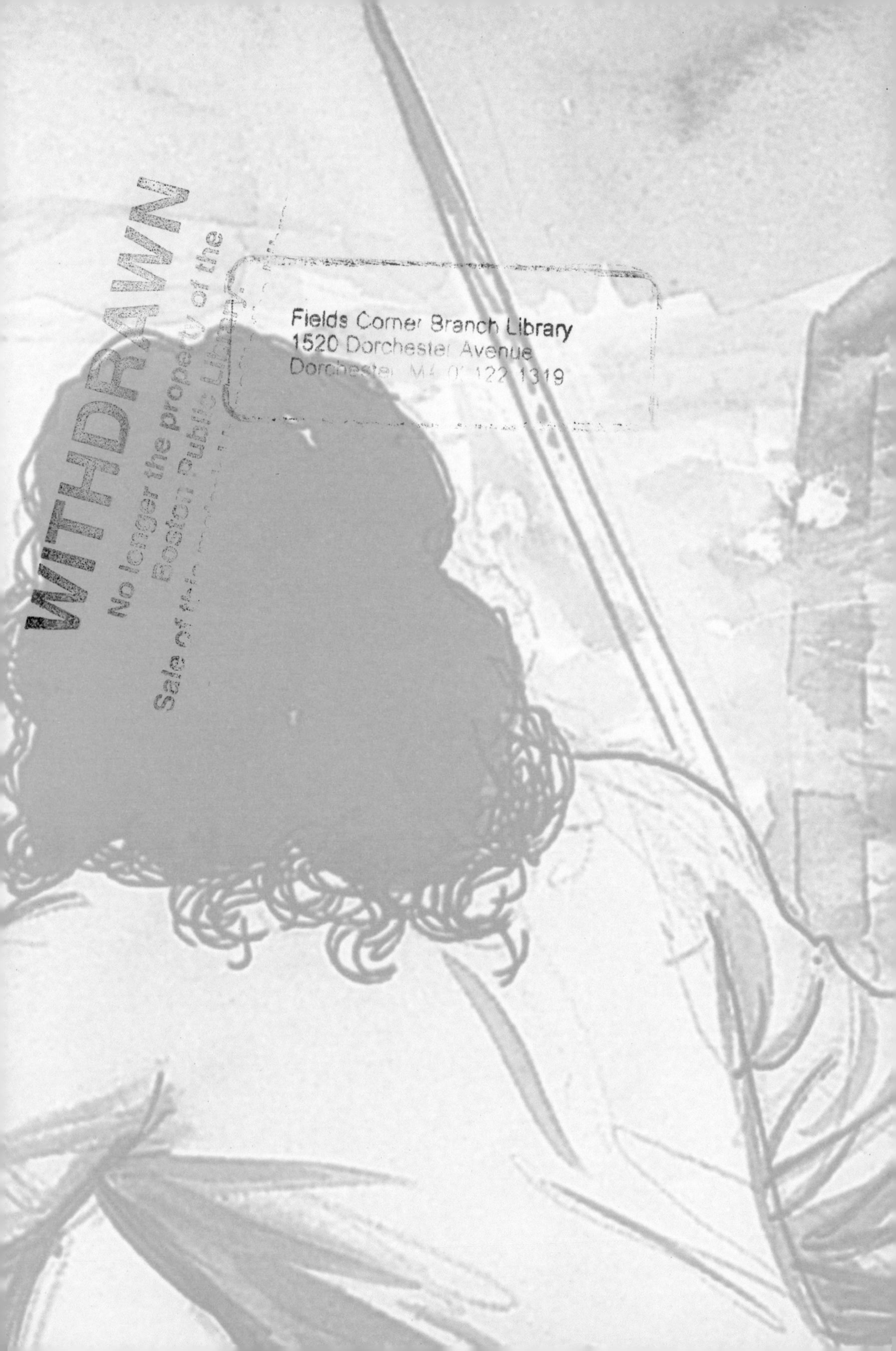